"Thank God, you're awake," Brandie said, dropping to her knees. **"Are you okay?"**

"Tell me what happened and why you're here. Was there a break-in?" Mitch asked.

"I...um..." Her eyes darted everywhere except directly at him.

Sign of a guilty conscience?

"Brandie? Did you see anything? Have you called the sheriff? And you still haven't said what brought you to the garage."

"How hard did they hit your head? Those are the most words you've ever said to me at one time before."

"Sorry."

"Don't be. I like the sound of your voice. Makes me feel safe." She twisted her fingers in the bottom of her shirt. "I got a phone call that the door was open. When I pulled up you were unconscious."

She had to have received a call or visit from the mystery man who'd jumped him. This entire time, he'd had his ear to the ground listening for pertinent news about someone helping the Mexican cartel.

He'd never suspected he might be working with the very person.

THE RANGER

Angi Morgan

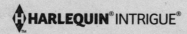

Thanks to everyone in the magic room: Jan, Janie, Lara, Jodi, Tish, Jen, Gina, Tyler Ann and Robin. Tim, thanks for doing the dishes. And Kourtney—who consistently amazes me—thank you so much for your help with this series.

Recycling programs for this product may not exist in your area.

ISBN-13: 978-0-373-69822-6

The Ranger

Copyright © 2015 by Angela Platt

This edition published by arrangement with Harlequin Books S.A.

For questions and comments about the quality of this book, please contact us at CustomerService@Harlequin.com.

Printed in U.S.A.

Angi Morgan writes Harlequin Intrigue novels "where honor and danger collide with love." She combines actual Texas settings with characters who are in realistic and dangerous situations. Angi and her husband live in north Texas, with only the four-legged "kids" left in the house to interrupt her writing. They recently began volunteering for a local Labrador retriever foster program. Visit her website, angimorgan.com, or hang out with her on Facebook.

Books by Angi Morgan

HARLEQUIN INTRIGUE

Visit the Author Profile page at Harlequin.com for more titles

CAST OF CHARACTERS

Mitch Striker—Undercover Texas Ranger working as a drifter mechanic at Junior's Garage. Is he getting too attached to his assignment?

Brandie Ryland—Manager of the Marfa Café and Junior's Garage. The town knows her tragic story of marrying before her husband shipped out and how he died overseas. But she has a secret.

Toby Ryland—Brandie's four-year-old son.

Bud & Olivia Quinn—Brandie's father and mother love their daughter and grandson. They own the Café and Junior's, and worked until Bud had a heart attack. They just want what's best for their daughter.

Cord McCrea—Texas Ranger and ranch owner, head of the newly formed West Texas task force. His wife is ranch owner Kate Danver McCrea.

Pete Morrison—Sheriff of Presidio County, Texas, and member of the joint West Texas task force. His fiancée is Andrea Allen.

Beth Conrad—DEA agent and member of the joint West Texas task force. Her fiancé is Nick Burke.

Nick Burke—Owner of the Rocking B Ranch and unofficial member of the joint West Texas task force. He's the best tracker in three counties.

Honey & Peach—Sisters who dispatch for the Presidio County Sheriff's Department.

Patrice Orlando—A woman who delivers messages for the drug smugglers/gunrunners known as the Chessmen.

Mr. King—A former professor turned smuggler who plays chess and uses innocent people to fulfill his obligations.

The Queen—The most powerful player on a chess board.

Chapter One

Mitch cracked one eyelid open, staring at pavement. The last thing he remembered was palming his .45 and soundlessly skirting the back wall of Junior's garage. He'd been about to open the office door, tripped and then nothing but stars. God bless 'em, but he'd seen enough pinpoints of light in the past couple of minutes to last a lifetime.

Texas Ranger Mitchell Striker had been an undercover mechanic in Marfa going on six months. Too long in his humble opinion, but no one asked him. He couldn't see a blasted thing from his position on the cement. He concentrated on the sounds around him. Shuffling of smooth-soled shoes inside the office. Papers falling to the floor. Excited breathing.

It didn't make sense that he'd fallen. If anything was out of place where he worked, he would have been the one to leave it there.

Nothing was ever left out of place. He hadn't tripped.

He'd been hit on the back of his head. If he concentrated any harder, he'd hear the lump pushing through his hair. Inching his left hand, minutely extending his arm, he tried to find his gun.

A noise like someone bumping the chair, followed by muffled voices awakened him from a light sleep in the back room. He'd come to the office but must not have been as quiet as he'd thought. The guy with the smooth shoes had gotten the drop on him.

"You didn't have to hit him with a wrench."

Mitch froze, recognizing the woman's voice. Daughter of the garage owner and his boss, Brandie Ryland. She should be at home with her son, not rustling through files in the middle of the night. Files she had access to anytime she asked in the daylight.

"What if you've seriously hurt him?"

"Good. We told you to clear him out for a while. Why's he here in the middle of the night? You got something on the side?"

Male voice with a bit of a northern nasal. Clearly not from south of the border or Texas.

"He's my mechanic and sleeps in the back room." Brandie moved next to him. Tiny bare feet, he could see she'd painted her toenails herself and had missed a spot on the outside of her pinky. The color was her, calm blue with festive glitter. She knelt beside him, and her toes were replaced with cartoon characters covering her knees.

"Where do you hide the cash around here?"

She wanted to rob her own garage? She didn't need muscle for that.

Cool, shaky hands gently parted the hair where he'd been hit. Just a lump or she would have hissed at the sight of blood. Mitch had seen her practically pass out when Toby had gashed his shin falling from his tricycle. She stroked his longish hair covering his face to tuck it behind his ear. He was forced to completely close his eyes and couldn't see where her partner was located.

"I don't keep cash here." Brandie was lying. Mitch knew she put it in the safe overnight and drove it to the bank after the breakfast crowd thinned out.

"I can't get it to work," the male voice accused, shaking something.

"I told you it wouldn't. We got rid of the phone line back here," she whispered. "Help me get Mitch to my car. I should take him to the hospital."

"You ain't for reals. For a bonk on the head? I ain't helping you do nothin'. You're lucky I didn't give him a kick or two in the face. What a waste of my time."

Kicking anywhere would wake him up and warrant a reaction.

"You need to leave. Tell him I was right and you shouldn't come out here."

Mitch risked cracking his lids again.

The points of well-polished, expensive shoes came toward them. Nice, not supermart quality and definitely not from around here. He was ready to take this guy down. But Brandie's fingers curling his hair around his ear didn't seem frightened, just nervous.

"I think he's waking up," fancy shoes said, inching closer.

If Mitch moved, would he put Brandie in danger? Was it worth potentially blowing his cover? His superiors would say no. He'd been Mitch the Mechanic for going on two years now. Yet, his personal answer was an emphatic yes. He couldn't let anything happen to Brandie.

She stood, her bare feet right next to his torso. He didn't need to open his eyes to know what she looked like. Tiny compared to him, she was a redheaded spitfire on most days. She stood up to problem customers by sweet-talking them into agreeing with her.

"You aren't going to touch him. I said leave and I meant it."

"It's amazin' anything gets done out here in this Texas hell hole. Back home we wouldn't think twice about gettin' rid of this guy. Anyway, a stinkin' mechanic ain't worth the trouble you'd cause me. But you should think about the next time you's asked for something. Maybe be more serious tryin' to get hold of it," the unidentified man threatened. "You know I'll be back when he needs somet'in' else. Oh, and, Brandie, you've got a really gorgeous kid. His blond hair really makes him easy to spot."

A light step over Mitch and the man—and his shoes—were clip-clopping out the back door and down the gravel drive.

"Leave my son out of this," she threw out the door behind him. "You can tell your boss if he has something to say, he can come here and deliver the message himself."

She paced a couple of times in the small office. On the trip away from him, he looked to see where her arms were. Yep, fingers digging into the side of her neck. She was worried.

As she should be.

"Threatening him was such a dumb move. What am I going to do if he does show up? And how am I going to explain this to you?" She vented, faced him and flung her hands toward him. "Or anyone else for that matter? At least you aren't bleeding. But I can't just leave you lying there. I'll be right back with the first-aid kit from the café."

Did she know he was conscious? He'd remained motionless, kept his breathing regular. She didn't stick around for confirmation, popping to her feet and running through the dark garage.

He rolled to his back, searching for his weapon. He took a quick look around the office. The bastard walking away must have taken it. He rubbed the lump on his head, cursing that a runt who threatened kids had gotten the drop on him. *He did have to use a wrench.* He heard Brandie's feet slapping against the concrete of the garage and quickly drew the door closed, locked it and then sank, resting against it.

The night sky actually lit up the outside more than the cloaked dark inside the shop. It was all those dang stars. Over two years undercover along the border and he still couldn't get used to the millions and millions of them.

"Thank God, you're awake," Brandie said, dropping to her knees again and riffling through the first-aid kit. "Are you okay? Maybe we should get you to the hospital in Alpine?"

"I should be asking you that. You don't look so good. How did you know you needed to come rescue me?" He rubbed his head and watched her carefully for any type of reaction. "Got any ice in there?"

"Let me get some from the café." She put a hand against the ground to stand.

He covered it, keeping her where she was. "Naw, it can wait. Tell me what happened and why you're here. Was there a break in? I thought I heard a noise, got up and then there's nothing."

"I...um..." Her eyes darted everywhere except directly at him.

Sign of a guilty conscience?

"Brandie? Did you see anything? Have you called the sheriff? And you still haven't said what brought you to the garage?"

"How hard did they hit your head? Those are the most words you've ever said to me at one time before."

"Sorry."

"Don't be. I like the sound of your voice. Makes me feel safe." She twisted her fingers in the bottom of the loose skimpy pink shirt. "I got a phone call that the door was open. When I pulled up you were unconscious."

"Where's your cell?" he asked, hiding his disappointment that she had to lie.

"Why?"

She had to have gotten a call or visit from the mystery man. She was barefoot and still in her pajamas. His superiors could get a warrant for a phone dump, but it was just easier to take a look. He couldn't alert her to why he wanted to know.

This entire time, he'd had his ear to the ground listening for pertinent news about someone helping the Mexican cartel. He'd never suspected he might be working for that very person. Brandie Ryland was a liar? He couldn't trust her. Didn't want to believe she'd been fooling him with a struggling single mother routine.

"I'm going to call the sheriff," he answered.

"Is it really necessary? I mean, it doesn't look like they took anything."

"It's up to you, but someone did hit me over the head. Knocked me out cold."

"Are you going to sue me or something?"

"Hell, no. I want to press charges when they catch the guy. What if he does it again? Let me call 9-1-1 and I'll deal with it."

She slid her hand away from his and stood. Her phone had been tossed to the back of the desk. While she searched for it she destroyed evidence by picking up the papers and putting them back exactly where her *friend* had shoved them aside.

He held his hand out for the phone.

"I can make the call. I'm the manager. It's my responsibility." She dialed. Left a message with the sheriff's department. "It'll be a little while before someone gets here. I should get you that ice."

He reached out and snagged her hand. "What's really going on, Brandie?"

"I don't know what you mean."

"If you're in trouble, I can try to help."

The phone rang. "Great. My parents. I should take this. I'm fine, Dad. Mitch got hit on the head. He's fine, too." She placed the phone between them and pushed speaker. "Mitch is here in case you'd like to ask him anything."

"What happened? Peach just called from the police station and said there'd been a robbery. What did they take?"

"Nothing that we can tell, sir." Only his pride after that runt of the litter got the drop on him.

"I don't know what you're doing at the café at this hour, little girl. Who's watching Toby? Oh, he's here? Well, how was I supposed to remember that?" he mumbled to someone in the background, probably his wife, Olivia. "We'll be right there."

Her parents would interrupt them in less than five minutes.

"I should get a shirt."

"That's probably a good idea. Mom hasn't seen that much muscle since we went to the car show in Abilene," Brandie teased.

"We were robbed and the lady makes jokes." Her hands circled her neck again, protecting herself or maybe a subconscious sign she felt like she was choking?

She waited at the garage entrance. He had to turn sideways through the door to pass. She looked so worried that his hands cupped both of her petite shoulders before he remembered she was now his primary suspect. She tilted her head back to get a look at him and he saw a tear silently fall before she brushed it away.

"What if something had happened to you?" she whispered.

"It'll take more than a lug wrench to keep me down." He wasn't good at joking or conversation. And exceptionally not good at being cared about. "I guess I better get that shirt."

She nodded. "How do you know they hit you with a lug wrench?"

Damn, he was slipping. "It's on the floor."

"Oh. Everything's just gotten so weird. I'm just really glad you're okay. I, um—"

The red and blue of police lights spun just outside the window.

"Brandie! You in there?" Bud Quinn shouted from the parking lot.

"Your dad got here fast." Mitch pointed toward the old storeroom where he bunked. "Hey, do you need a…a shirt?"

"Oh, my gosh. I…" She wrapped her arms across her breasts, hiding the pert nipples. "Yes, please."

"I'll be right back."

He grabbed two shirts and his shoes, hanging back while Brandie explained things to her father. After their initial hug and his "thank God you're okay," Brandie's dad was all business and confronting the deputy and then the sheriff before he made it through the door.

Sheriff Pete Morrison had been on Mitch's back from his first day in town, keeping a close eye on his movements. Admittedly, Mitch had come into Marfa a self-proclaimed drifter looking for a job. This incident wouldn't make it easier to get around unnoticed. At least Morrison didn't look the type to try to run him out of town.

The deceit was a necessary evil. No one could know he was a Texas Ranger. Mitch would find the rat—or rat*ette*—and move on without anyone knowing. It was his job and he'd move up and down the border as long as the cover held.

He watched the men in the parking lot from inside the garage. The window opened toward the main road. Just a standard-looking gas station with a two-bay garage.

"That pole you're leaning on used to be covered in grease." Brandie handed him ice wrapped with a bar towel.

He shrugged, knowing it had taken a full day to clean it up. "I didn't have a lot to do until word got around I could tune an engine."

"I wish I could give you a raise."

Would she offer him money to keep his mouth shut? Was that dread creeping into his mind that she might actually be the cartel's contact? His job would be over if she was supplying the information. He could move on to the next assignment. Leave.

There was no way she was responsible for the drug and gun shipments getting across the border without detection. She couldn't be. His head was ready to memorize her words and something else grounded him to the pole he'd worked hard to clean up.

"I like it here." The word *amazed* passed through his mind. First that he'd admitted it out loud and second that it was true.

"That's good because I'm paying you more than I can afford as it is. Dad and I argue about it all the time. Thank goodness nothing was stolen or I'd never hear the end of it." She pulled the T-shirt over her pajama top and greeted the sheriff.

Funny, he didn't remember handing it to her. Just like he didn't remember exactly when he'd realized he was glad she wasn't married. Damn, he needed to catch this informant and move on before something emotional happened to him.

Chapter Two

Brandie was dead on her feet. The only real crowd the café had was at breakfast and, of course, it was her morning to open. Between Rey's threats and his minion's visit, she hadn't caught a wink of sleep. Zubict's name and northern accent was enough proof for her that Rey had expanded his association.

Her feet were dragging, and she felt emotionally bruised. Mitch, her father and the sheriff had spoken to her like she should know more than she'd told them. It didn't matter that she did. She'd never given them reason to doubt her before.

"I can handle the café if you want some shut-eye," Mitch said just behind her.

Rey and his men had bothered her with infrequent phone calls until two weeks ago when the visits began. Her parents hadn't picked up on the additional stress. She thought she'd hidden it from everyone, but the concern in Mitch's expression made her doubt she could hide anything from him for long.

"I'm fine. Really." She had just enough time to pick up Toby, get them both dressed, drop him at day care and head back for morning setup.

Mitch put a hand on hers as she unlocked the café door

for the cook. "I can take Toby by the day care then. That is, if you trust me."

His hand was strong and oh so warm—even through two T-shirts earlier. They'd probably touched more in the past couple of hours than the entire time he'd been working there. His touch had a calming effect on her that she was really enjoying.

"He's at my mom's, remember? Besides, you're the one who should be getting some rest. Is your head okay? Why don't you keep the garage closed this morning or take the entire day off? I'll get Sadie to bring you a breakfast special before she opens." He'd already saved her once, whether he knew it or not. Even lying unconscious on the floor had stopped Zubict from acting on what his eyes suggested each time he showed up. It gave her the creeps.

She slowly withdrew the key from the front bolt, her hand still covered by one of the most mysterious men she'd ever known. *Wait!* Tobias Ryland had been mysterious once and look where that had landed her. She glanced at her hand, and Mitch dropped it.

"I appreciate the offer, I really do. But this is my responsibility and I'll see it through."

"You got it. I'm going to hit the shower and grab a protein drink. Don't bother Sadie's routine. I'd rather— She's sort of— Seriously, I—" He walked to the gas station entrance seeming a bit flustered at the thought of meeting her newest waitress.

I sure do hope they aren't a thing. She got another whiff of his wonderful scent.

How? Oh, yes, she had his shirt around her. Extralarge and yet there wasn't an ounce of fat on the man. At her average height she felt like a midget next to him. He was well over six feet. She hadn't figured out if he dwarfed men by his height or just his presence.

Whatever it was, she wasn't alone. Sadie and the rest of the staff had taken notice. The high school boys she used for dishwashers never opened their mouths when he stood guard at the door. *Stood guard?* Yes, that's how he presented himself. He never really appeared...casual.

Mitch didn't seem to talk much and offered his opinion even less. Maybe that was why when he did offer, she listened. He made suggestions about the garage and waited for her to respond, to think about it. Unlike Glen Yost, the last mechanic who went to her father with every problem and potential scheme to get customers.

When her dad gave orders, Mitch responded that she was the one who had hired him and had stated—not bragged—that it was his skill that brought in business. And he was right. The garage was no longer a liability. She was grateful to him, but she couldn't take advantage of his kindness to drop Toby at his school. The old-fashioned cola clock above the café door was straight up on the hour. She'd be late, but no, she couldn't impose even when it would clearly help.

She wouldn't ask her parents to drop Toby at day care, either. She'd hear endless advice about how to manage her life better. Most likely they'd keep him at their house instead of taking him to day care. But the most important reason was that she honestly missed him and wanted that morning connection with her son. A brand-new day presented itself with enormous possibilities. Neither of them were normally bogged down with problems or frustrations. So she'd pick Toby up and desperately try to get her morning under control.

"Hi, Brandie. I heard you had some excitement around here this morning. Did they get away with anything?"

Sadie stowed her purse next to the safe in the storeroom. She sashayed to the coffeemaker, now perking and gurgling the first of its many pots for customers.

"Mitch seems to have interrupted them before they could make off with something important." She hated lying, but this was only half a lie. He really did interrupt Zubict.

"Oh, that poor man. Does he need someone to take care of him today? So is Mitch a dream without his shirt on? I heard he got caught in just his boxers."

Sadie popped a hip to one side, flipping her dress and showing off her legs. She constantly said her calves were her best feature and that she could give anyone a pair if they attended her aerobic classes in Alpine. Brandie had tried to find it one day while she was shopping, but hadn't had any luck. It wouldn't have mattered, she couldn't afford to attend anyway.

"It's amazing that you've already heard anything. But please don't repeat that rumor. He was wearing jeans."

Brandie was lucky to have Sadie Dillon, even if it was for only three days a week. A flirty thirtysomething who was an adequate cook. She could make a lot more money anywhere else, but said she enjoyed the company here. Thank goodness they all got along. Competent help was one of the reasons her dad had turned the management of the café and garage over to her.

"Did you count to see if he had a six-pack? Were his abs as yummy as I think they are?"

"I did not look at his chest," she lied terribly, giggling like a teenage girl behind her hand.

"Oh, yes, you did. Brandie Ryland, you are such a tease." She switched legs, popping her opposite hip, smacking a piece of gum and twirling a dark brown curl just below her ear. "I guess you didn't have time to take a picture."

"Of course not. Oh, gosh, it's getting late." She accepted a to-go cup of coffee from Sadie. "I've got to get Toby."

"Good thing he was with your parents last night."

"If he'd been at home, I would have gotten Dad to come up here and I wouldn't be late. I better run."

Almost to her parents' home, her mother phoned and volunteered to take Toby to day care. Brandie didn't ask for favors, but when her mother volunteered, she accepted. She hated not to see him. He always put her in a good mood. Getting back to the café earlier would help.

Not making the stop at her parents' would speed up her timetable tremendously. Dropping Toby would only take twenty minutes, but she always allowed a good half hour to pick her son up. She'd answer her mother's questions and listen to her advice on how she'd run the café until her father's heart attack had changed everything.

Brandie had too much to think about and didn't need to dwell on how her life had changed in the blink of an eye.

At the moment, all she had to do was shower and get back on the job. She didn't have to worry about anything or anyone. She sighed a deep release and was immediately surrounded by Mitch's manly scent. She'd gone an entire four or five minutes without thinking about him. He could have been hurt much worse and it would have been her fault.

She had a good life and no one, especially Rey King, was going to take it from her. She'd drawn a line in the sand this morning. It wouldn't take long to see who he'd send to cross over.

Had she really thought that she had nothing to worry about? Whatever was in the garage, those scum buckets needed Mitch to leave. The suggestion this morning was for Brandie to ask him to stay at her place.

That was absurd. She was his boss. They didn't have

any attraction to each other…at least none she could act on. Stop. It would do no good to lie to herself. She was strongly attracted to Mitch Striker. Who wouldn't be?

She'd counted his abs all right. It had taken a great deal of willpower to caress his head for injuries instead of his chest.

MITCH COULD BE in the middle of nowhere five minutes after leaving most of the towns where he'd been stationed for undercover work. It made it easy to meet handlers and made it difficult to find the bastards breaching the border.

After refusing Brandie's offer of a day off, he'd contacted his counterpart on this operation. They could meet at noon instead of the dead of night.

Mitch had worked with a different Ranger in each of the cities where he'd landed a job. Most places he stayed two or three months, tops. Presidio County's problems were bigger.

Officially a part of a task force set up by the Homeland Security Customs and Border Protection Office, he was the member no one knew about. With the exception of Cord McCrea. This task force had been attempting to bring down a well-organized gun- and drug-smuggling operation for several months.

The West Texas task force had already caught two criminal leaders and stopped two major gun shipments to Mexico.

The Rangers believed someone had picked up the pieces of those organizations. So quickly that it seemed he'd planned their demise. Each successful takedown was important, but within weeks the smugglers had another operation up and running. And now the new principal player wanted something from Brandie.

He'd never seen this place in the daylight and didn't

think Cord would use his truck—one that everyone in the county could spot. But he still watched the road instead of the trail behind him. Then he heard a horse galloping toward him.

"I've been looking in the wrong direction. For some reason, I didn't think you'd be riding up on a horse."

"I do live on a ranch," Cord said, dropping the reins next to the car. "Didn't you know this was Kate's property?"

"I figured. Did you bring it?"

"Your conk on the head has made the rounds about town. Kate even asked me about it." Cord took a holstered weapon from his saddlebag. "I only had a spare SIG. I have to report your Glock missing."

"I know. It's one of the reasons I didn't mention it to our friend the sheriff. Sure wish you could let Pete in on this soiree. He might threaten me less with a jail stay. It might even make our conversations a little more productive." Mitch leaned on the old car he used while undercover. He'd worked on the engine until it purred.

"I will when the time's right. I'd like to keep the fact you're on the task force under wraps as long as possible. You need anything besides the gun?"

"Some background on Brandie Ryland and her family."

"What's Brandie— Wait a minute, are you saying that Brandie hit you over the head with a pipe?"

"It was a lug wrench and no. She let a guy into the shop, and *he* hit me over the head. I heard a noise and was eating concrete before I saw his face." He rubbed his chin, which had begun to feel as bruised as his lump. "I did manage a good look at his shoes. Not boots. Real nice, not local stock if you know what I mean. Had a bit of a northern accent."

Mitch had met Cord in street clothes many times. This time, he looked more the part of a cowboy. A Stetson that had seen better days, but he wouldn't retire. He'd overheard stories at the café about that hat and how even a winter blizzard couldn't blow it off his head.

"This guy threatened Toby just before he left," he added. "I don't think it's the first time, either."

"That's not good. You think Brandie's the informant we're trying to find?" Cord asked while patting his horse's thick neck.

"I don't know. Maybe. There are a couple of other new people in town. The Dairy Queen took on a new face and Brandie's waitress would hear a lot of talk."

"Anything pointing you in their direction?"

"Not anything I can pinpoint." He didn't care for indecisiveness.

The more he looked away from Brandie, the more it seemed he shouldn't.

Every instinct in him told him to protect Brandie, that she hadn't been capable of fooling him for six months. Yet he had to be truthful. If Brandie was guilty, there was nothing he could do to save her.

"I'll add that I agree Brandie doesn't seem the type. Not from what I've picked up on. It sounded like the cartel might have found a way to force her to cooperate with threats or something in her past."

"I'll check with headquarters." Cord flipped the end of the reins he held and dismounted.

"Is there a *but* in that statement?"

"I don't see her betraying all the people around here. This is a close community. I've known Brandie's parents a while now. Kate's known the Quinn family her whole life."

"I'll remind you, sir, of what you wrote when you requested someone to come in undercover. You wanted a new set of eyes to look over the people out here—including your friends. That's why I'm here. A new look. I'll stay close to her and see if I can pick up on anything."

"You've been darn close to her for six months. Hell, you live there." The horse nickered and tossed its head at Cord's tension. "Take it easy, Ginger. Wait. Don't tell me you're going to saddle up next to her. As in date Brandie? She hasn't dated anyone since moving home."

"It's the only way. She was on the verge of telling me something before the sheriff showed up this morning. I think she'll confide in me if I can get her away from the café."

"Just be careful. I like Brandie. She's bounced back after a rough go of it when her husband died. If she's involved… Honestly, I just don't believe she is." Cord dropped his head enough that his hat covered his face.

"That's the rancher, not the Ranger talking." But it was good to know his instincts about Brandie weren't just because he was attracted to her. "I'll get to the truth. You're aware that I don't prejudge."

"Fine." He mounted, his feisty horse kicked up dust as it turned in a circle then settled down. "You sure you're okay and don't need to have your head checked out?"

"Naw, two aspirin took care of the pain." Mitch had his hand on the door handle of his old sedan.

"If you're going to *date* Brandie, I'm officially reminding you not to sleep with her. You shouldn't get involved with a suspect."

"What kind of a man do you think I am?"

"One with eyes. That young woman is attractive in more ways than you can count, and her kid has a serious daddy crush on you. I mean that in a good way, Mitch. He needs an authority figure. I don't think you meant to, but you're providing it when you spend time with him." He pushed his hat lower on his forehead. "Just be careful. For both your sakes."

"Careful. Got it."

Mitch had never thought of the way Toby liked hanging out with him as a *daddy crush*. But come to think about it, he'd done exactly the same thing with his father on more than one occasion as he'd grown up. His dad had taught him everything he knew about repairing a car. It had been their thing every other weekend. The only thing that got them through the first years after his parents divorced.

He could act the role of a concerned boyfriend without blowing his cover. He did need to be careful, though. He could really get into playing both roles—temporary daddy and boyfriend.

Chapter Three

"What a day." Brandie wiped the last booth and dropped the wet vinegar-soaked cloth over her shoulder. *Exhausted* seemed like a word with too much energy. She had none. "I've never had the stamina to pull all-nighters, back in college or when Toby was an infant. I feel terrible."

The evening cook had finished his cleanup and headed for home. Brandie looked through the serving window where her mechanic put the last of the dishes away.

"I sure am glad you could help out this afternoon, Mitch. I had no idea we'd get busy after I sent the staff home. But I think we made bread money this month."

"Not a problem. Do buses normally just pull up outside with no warning?"

"I gave the driver our number. He's going to check with us next time. He said he thought his charter company had called. Thanks for suggesting some of the customers shop before eating."

She gathered the bills from the cash register and went to the back room to place the bag in the safe. She'd make the deposit on her day off or take a break when one of the part-timers worked.

"For a morning that started out questionable," Mitch said from the front of the café, "it turned out well for you."

He stepped away from the jukebox and her favorite song started playing.

It brought a smile to her lips every time she heard it. Tonight was no exception. Especially since Mitch had chosen something she liked. So he'd noticed what music she played when she was here alone? *Duh. He could hear it in his room at the back of the garage.*

"You're absolutely right. A bad start but an awesome finish." She took the hand he extended and swung into his arms. When their fingers touched she thought about Rey wanting her to get Mitch away from the garage. Only a split-second thought because she was ready for a moment of not thinking at all. A moment to let her mind rest and just feel nice swaying to the music.

Feeling Mitch's arms around didn't hurt, either. He was an expert dancer and it was so easy to lean her ear against his chest and let him weave them between the tables. She could sweep and mop early in the morning.

Right now, it felt wonderful being held by someone taller than herself. She loved having her son's arms around her and missed him terribly on days like today when she worked from open to close. But there was something about a man guiding you around a dance floor, trusting him to protect you.

"I can't remember the last time I went dancing. Probably before Toby was born."

"No talking. Just enjoy the music."

Brandie relaxed and let him lead with confidence. The next song was country swing. With gentle nudges at her waist, his strong hands had her performing fancy dance moves she'd never dreamed of before. When the song was over they were both laughing, and she leaned in to hug him.

"That felt so good." She craned her neck backward to look up into his eyes.

"Then we need to do it again." He leaned toward her.

Brandie didn't dodge him. His lips were amazingly soft for a man, but still firm. Tall, lean, comforting, protective, strong…all were good words to describe him. The scruff from his five o'clock shadow teased her cheek, and she kissed him back, drinking in his taste and trying to remember the last exciting thrill she'd had.

Then it hit her. The last dance and intimate kiss had been saying goodbye. She jerked back, bumping into a table and scooting the chair a little across the floor. "I… um…I'm afraid I've given you the wrong impression, Mitch."

"It was just a kiss. I doubt your boyfriend will get upset."

Not a boyfriend. But Rey would be more upset that she hadn't let the kiss continue and progress to an overnight stay at her house.

"Oh, I'm not dating anyone. I can't. I don't have any intention of dating at all. I have a son to raise. There's just no time for a relationship."

"I wouldn't think a dance and kiss meant we had a relationship. But let's say it does. What's wrong with a man in your life who understands your commitments and doesn't want to take you away from them? I like Toby. He's a terrific kid. You've done a great job." He took a step, pushed his hand through his hair.

He had a very frustrated look on his face that didn't match the complimentary words he spoke aloud.

"Thanks, that means a lot. I better lock up now." She fished the keys from her pocket and was ready to think more about their moment once she got home.

He snagged her hand and twirled her back in front of him. "You didn't answer my question. What's the big deal about having a little fun? I'd love it if Toby could come, too."

"It's going to just break his heart when you leave." Hers was going to ache a little, too. "I can't do that to him." *To us.*

"Here I am asking you on a date and you've got me leaving town, breaking a kid's heart. How did that happen? You firing me for asking the boss out?"

"No, of course not." The bell over the door rang, letting them both know someone had walked into the café. Mitch released her.

"Sorry, we're closed, man. I must have forgotten to turn the sign," Mitch said.

She froze in her tracks. She hadn't seen Rey King in three years and then only for a passing moment while she'd been in Alpine. Even bothering her like he had for the past six months, he'd never made the trip to Marfa. He'd always sent one of his men with a message of veiled threats about divulging the secrets her parents wanted desperately to keep.

"Hey, buddy," Mitch said from over her head. "Really, we're closed. Cook's gone home. Not even a slice of pie left."

Mitch took her arm and gently pulled her behind the counter.

"How about a latte?" Rey requested as he sat on one of the bar stools.

What was he doing here? *No. No. No!* He couldn't invade her business. Fright, powerful and swift, forced the happiness of a few moments ago into the recess of her everything. What could he want with her? Even if she said he should ask her himself, she never imagined that he would. Especially here. Now.

"If we served latte—which we don't—I just told you we're closed," Mitch said with force.

She watched as his hand moved under the counter to a bat they kept there for emergencies. She, on the other hand, could only watch. Words... Movement... Both had temporarily left her paralyzed.

"Mitch, I don't think Mr. King is here for coffee."

The man on her side of the counter jerked his head her direction, surprise on his face. The man responsible for her current problems tipped his head toward the door where two men stood, hands inside their jackets, staying their actions. She could only assume their fingers were ready to pull guns and shoot.

"How's your head?" Rey asked Mitch.

Mitch's eyes narrowed, his eyebrows drew into a straight line as his fingers wrapped around the grip of the bat. She crossed over to him and patted his hand, moving the bat into her possession and giving him an assuring smile. Or at least she hoped she did no matter how stiff it felt.

"It's okay. Can you make sure the rest of the doors are locked?"

"Yeah, Mitch, go away like a good boy. Brandie and I have some catching up to do."

After a threatening glare directed toward first Rey and then his men, Mitch left. It surprised her that he left so quickly. But she had asked him to secure the other doors. Rey might have brought more than just two thugs with weapons, and Mitch seemed like the sort of man who would think that direction.

"Why are you here?"

"What? An old friend can't come for a visit?" He nodded toward the door, and one of the men left. The other turned the lock and watched the lot out front.

"You aren't my friend. I don't know how many times I have to tell you that." She said the words as bravely as she could, but didn't feel very courageous. She couldn't predict anything about this man and had no way to stop him.

"Don't push my patience, girl." He grabbed the front of her apron across her breasts and tugged. "You sent an invitation and I accepted."

The apron loop behind her head kept her from getting free. Her face inched closer to him across the counter. The bat bounced to the floor at her feet. Now painfully on her tiptoes, Rey kept pulling until she could smell the wretched onions he'd had with his dinner.

"I don't know what you mean," she eked out, trying to be brave and not turn away.

"Weren't my instructions clear to get your *boy* out of here so my men could reclaim what's rightfully mine?"

He smashed his lips against hers. She jerked back as much as allowed, far enough to get the word *stop* out before he jerked her lips to his again. His hard, punishing mouth took everything wonderful about kissing and turned it into a horrible experience.

"Enough. Let her go."

Mitch shoved Rey's shoulder with a thick pipe, and Brandie slid back to her feet. Rey stood and held his hand in the air, signaling for the man behind him to stop.

"No need for violence, friends. Stand down. I will come back another time when you aren't entertaining." Rey winked at her and straightened his expensive suit.

"That's not about to happen while I'm here," Mitch said. "I imagine you sent the guy who hit me on the head this morning. Tell him I'd like to know where he got his shoes."

Rey perked up. He tried to look casual about it, but Mitch made him nervous. It was evident in the way he buttoned his jacket and gave directions to his guards in Spanish.

"Sweet Brandie...*au revoir* until next time."

"There won't be a next time, buddy. Or your face will be on a wanted poster. Got it?"

Rey didn't acknowledge Mitch. Just turned his back and left. Mitch followed to the door and secured it.

"What the hell did that guy want? Is he trying to shake you down?"

"No. I need to warn my parents. Rey isn't the type to walk out of here and do nothing." She picked up her cell. Her hands were shaking so much she could barely tap just one number. She should just go, but she couldn't think. What did she need? "My keys. Is the door locked? Yes, I saw you lock it behind him."

"Brandie." Mitch caught her between his arms and pulled her to his chest. "Catch your breath, then we go. I can't help you if you don't tell me what's going on."

"Mom's not answering. You don't think he'd really kidnap or hurt them, do you?" She saw the answer in his eyes. "You do." She shoved at his sturdy chest. "I'm leaving. Right now."

"And I'm going with you. No discussion." He dangled her keys in front of her face. "Who is that guy, and don't give me any bunk about not knowing him. You're scared of him."

"I'll tell you on the way."

"You're not waiting on me. Cars are out back."

He pointed to the rear garage entrance. Mitch stopped her before she turned the knob. He tossed her the keys and pulled a gun from the top file drawer.

"Has that been on the premises all this time?" She couldn't imagine Mitch owning a gun or that he'd been playing with Toby in this very room.

"Shh. Let's get to the car. Then we'll talk." He held the gun and searched through the windows like a professional.

Professional what?

Something had changed, and suddenly she could definitely picture him with a gun. There was Mitch the silent mechanic and Mitch the fun guy twirling her around the café. Then the almost shy Mitch who'd asked her on a date. Then there was this version. He pivoted around corners like the cops on television. At any point she thought he'd start giving her hand signals to stop and advance.

It wasn't funny. Nor was it supposed to be. She was confused by meeting all of this man's personalities on the same day. She watched his eyes looking everywhere. How he tensed at the sound of a car passing on the street.

"We go through the door. You lock it and I've got your back. Is your car locked?" She answered with a shake of her head. "Great. Just great. You're too dang trusting, Brandie. We'll take my car. They might not have known which one if they were going to rig something to blow or break down. You're driving. The keys are in my front right pocket."

Back to her, he blocked her from any potential threat, holding the gun down, but ready to shoot. He turned his hip for her to have access to his keys. She couldn't dig in the man's pockets.

Forget what she'd normally think or normally do. They might already have Toby. Brandie followed his instructions.

In other circumstances, fishing in his pockets would be an intimate gesture. He remained silent, cocking his head to the side when a car slowed and its occupants looked closely at the gas pumps.

"We move to the car, you keep the alley on one side and me between you and the street. Got it?"

"Sure." Her insides started jumping. Whoever this man really was, he was there to protect her. The frightening thing was that she needed protecting at all. She lived in a sleepy little town that probably wouldn't be there if not for the phenomenon of lights in the sky.

Hands shaking, she unlocked his old four-door sedan and got behind the wheel. As soon as he was in the car, she spun gravel as she left the garage lot, totally not expecting the powerful engine.

"Take it easy there. We don't need the locals pulling us over," he directed, placing the pistol in his lap. "Start talking, please."

"Are you an undercover cop?" That had to be the only explanation.

"No."

"Is Mitch Striker your real name?"

"Almost. We don't have much time, Brandie. I need to know everything."

"No. I appreciate the help. But if you aren't a cop you may be working for Rey to see if I'm going to spill my guts the first time he walks through the door."

"First time for him? But there have been others. Like the guy with the fancy shoes this morning."

"Nope. I'm not talking." She shook her head and turned off the main road. "I think someone's following us." Brandie had seen the lights in the rearview mirror. On the highway through town she might not have paid attention, but this car hung back just far enough to make her wonder.

"Yeah, it's waiting to see which way you turn—right to your parents' or left to your house. We should get to your dad's place."

They turned the last corner, and the car following stopped half a block behind them.

"Pull over. Now."

She jerked the wheel right and slammed on the brakes.

"Why did you want me to stop? What if— Just the possibility of something happening to Toby is making me sick."

"I know what I'm doing, Brandie, but I'll need your help."

Mitch slid the car into Park and switched off the ignition. Something in the calm directness of his voice made her listen when all she wanted to do was throw open the car door and run to the house to see if her family was okay.

She nodded and dropped her head to the wheel. "Why aren't they answering the phone? Are his men already inside?"

"I need you to do two things. First, you call 9-1-1. Ask them to dispatch Pete and tell him some of the men he's looking for are at your parents'. That's it. Hang up after." He reached into the backseat and raised a blanket, pulling a backpack from the floorboard.

"You *are* a cop. Where arc you going? You're leaving me here? What if they already have Toby?" Each word dried her throat a little more, making it difficult to sound confident. Her insides knotted, her hands shook with fright and anger. Holding on to the steering wheel was the only thing keeping her inside the car. She removed her foot from the brake, finally realizing the car wouldn't go anywhere.

"I'm giving my word. If something's happened to Toby, I guarantee that I'll find the bastards and make them pay. If he's gone, I'll find him and bring him home." He covered her hand with his left and pulled a second gun from the glove box with his right.

Until she knew her son was safe, her heart would be controlling her actions. She searched his eyes. He meant every word and then some. She didn't care who he worked for as long as he'd defend Toby.

"What's the second thing?" she whispered, afraid with

every second that she'd break down, melting into a puddle of hysteria.

"Whatever's happened, I need you to keep quiet about this Rey guy."

"That doesn't make sense. Rey King is the only person who's threatened me. If something bad has happened, he's the prime suspect. The sheriff will need to know."

What would she tell them? That a respected man from Alpine had been sending men for unknown reasons to her café, searching for something she wasn't aware existed? She could just hear the conversation with Pete where every answer she provided was a resounding *I don't know*.

"I need this guy to think his threats have worked. Trust me."

"Just admit that you're a cop."

He shook his head. "I'll explain everything later. Right now—" the engine varoomed to life as he turned the key "—we need to find out who's following and why."

"So what do I do?"

"Act natural and trust me."

It had been a long time since she'd done either. The last time she'd trusted someone hadn't worked out. At all. In spite of her instincts screaming at her to do otherwise, maybe her heart wanted to believe that this man was different.

"I'll trust you, Mitch." *Until you give a reason not to.* "But if Toby's injured or gone, I'll keep Rey's name out of it for my own purposes. I know how to use a gun, too."

Chapter Four

I know how to use a gun, too. Mitch knew that calm, kill 'em with kindness Brandie Ryland didn't make that threat lightly. She meant every unspoken word and would kill Rey King—whoever he was—if anything happened to Toby.

Nothing was going to happen to the kid. Mitch wouldn't let it. As he thought the words, he knew how futile they were. Many times fate stepped in no matter how many precautions you took to prevent it.

He watched her reverse his car in next to her dad's truck. Good idea, they could leave faster if things went sideways. The car that had followed them idled at the corner. If Brandie looked at it, no one could see her eyes from this distance. Surprise had to be on his side. He needed to make this quick.

Mitch had several sets of zip cuffs in his back pocket, two extra clips for the weapon in his palm and enough adrenaline for a battle. These guys didn't act like they'd seen him get out of the car. He'd left under the cover of darkness, having disconnected the dome light as soon as the vehicle had been issued to him.

Run! He did. Leaving his spot on the opposite side of the road from Brandie, he was able to catch these guys while they watched her walk into her dad's home. If someone was inside, he'd deal with them next.

Right now, he jerked the passenger door open, slugged the goon dressed in black in the jaw, knocking him into the driver. The driver honked the horn twice. *Damn it.* That probably was a signal for whoever was making a move on the house. He shoved the passenger onto the driver to keep him from putting the car into gear and taking off. Both men went for their weapons inside their jackets.

"Hold it. You don't want to pull on me. I'm not used to this SIG. No safety. I'm a Glock man, myself. I hate it when guns go off sooner than I anticipate. Now, push your hands through the wheel and lace your fingers under the steering column."

The driver followed his directions. The passenger pushed off his friend and tried to head butt Mitch, but Mitch was faster, shoving the man's ear into the dashboard.

"I didn't give you permission to move. Behave yourself." He stuck the barrel of the SIG next to the man's head, tossing him the zip cuffs. "First your friend, then you."

Neither man had said a word. Not a complaint or a curse. They were more concerned with watching the house. He grabbed a cell phone, which had landed on the floorboard, and their guns, adding them to his bag. Then he took the keys and yanked the nylon circles tight against their hairy wrists until they winced.

"I don't suppose you're going to tell me what's waiting in that house." Silence. "I didn't think so." He took the roll of duct tape from his bag, tore two sufficient pieces and silenced both men. "The sheriff will be here shortly to collect you."

Mitch covertly ran the block to the Quinns' house. He expected the lights and sirens of the sheriff or a deputy at any moment. He was counting on the distraction. As long as he got into the house and prevented any harm from coming to Brandie's family, he'd feel successful.

The house had plenty of large windows for him to get a good glimpse of the situation inside. He'd been correct. The car horn had been a signal to let Mr. Fancy Shoes know Brandie had arrived.

Bud and Olivia were tied to kitchen chairs, blindfolded. Safe. If they didn't witness him in the house, his cover could be saved. No talking. No contact with the Quinns. He needed to make certain Fancy Shoes couldn't identify him, either.

A complicated rescue. Where were the cops?

Brandie stood just inside the front door. Fancy Shoes held her at gunpoint, but from his position near the hallway he would be able to see movement at both the front and rear doors. If Mitch entered either way, Fancy Shoes could shoot all three adults.

Where was Toby? Just as he asked himself, he could hear Brandie asking the same thing. He had to get inside that house. He walked the perimeter, looking for an open window. Bingo! He lifted and removed the screen, then shoved the old four-pane window up without a lot of sound or trouble.

And the cops? Marfa wasn't big enough to take more than ten minutes to get from anywhere to anywhere. So where were they? Mitch slid his bag to the floor. He could hear a muted argument and pulled himself over the windowsill.

He cracked the bedroom door open enough to see a hallway and sitting right on the edge of the pool of light from the living room, just beyond the line of sight of a machine pistol, was Toby. His little thumb was stuck in his mouth, something Mitch had never seen the five-year-old do. His bedroom was at the end of the hall where a projection lamp still spun, shooting images of airplanes on the wall.

Mitch still wasn't in a position to charge into the room, guns ablazin'. He wouldn't be saving anyone. He needed the distraction he thought the arrival of the police would cause. Then it hit him. For whatever reason, Brandie hadn't called 9-1-1. He couldn't, his phone was in the car.

He was on his own.

As he inched through the door, Mitch put a finger to his lips. Hopefully, Toby would see it and remain quiet. When he went past the hall entrance, Brandie would see him. Her reaction could give him away, and Fancy Shoes could react badly.

"Come on, Zubict. I want to make sure Toby's okay. Can't you do that?"

Fancy Shoes had a name—Zubict. Had to be real; who would ever call themselves that?

"The kid's asleep. I ain't touched him. Don't mean I'll keep it that way. So you best behave yourself." Zubict leaned against the wall.

"What does Rey expect from me?"

"Anything he needs. Like getting rid of the new guy. We calls, you tell us what Rey needs to know. Then no more problems and we don't go through this again."

Mitch wanted the conversation to exonerate Brandie. He wanted her to be an innocent bystander in whatever plan was going on around her. The more he listened, the less it seemed like she was an unwilling participant.

"Are they at the garage now? Aren't you worried about Mitch?"

"The other fellas will take care of that jerk. Don't worry that pretty little red head about none of it." The gun relaxed in his hand a bit, drooping, pointing toward the floor. "Just relax. It ain't none of your business."

"Until the next time."

Toby stood, acting like he was going to his mother. Mitch put up his hands, indicating for the little boy to stop. He had to get across the wooden floor without making any sound. He inched himself into Brandie's view. Half his face could be seen before he made eye contact. The woman didn't miss a beat.

"If you tell me what you're looking for, I could tell you where it's at and maybe they won't tear my place up. Just like I told you this morning."

Mitch cleared the hall entrance and scooped Toby up. He had to cover the kid's mouth to keep him from talking.

"That's up to Rey and he didn't seem much interested in any deals," Zubict said.

Mitch couldn't see anything as he squeezed through the opening to Toby's room and continued to the closet on the far wall.

"I can't go in there, Mr. Mitch. Gramma Ollie will pank me."

"Your Gramma wants you to hide in the sewing closet. No spankings. I promise." He whispered, then opened the door without a creak, dumped the laundry basket of scrap material onto the floor and set Toby in the basket. "We're going to hide from the bad man. Okay, Toby? Can you stay as quiet as a mouse?" The little boy nodded. "Great. I'm going to cover you up and it's going to look like your Gramma's sewing. Don't be afraid. I'll be right back. Promise."

He left the closet open a crack so it wouldn't be pitch-black. *Time to kick some bad-guy ass*. He was about to swing around the corner and eliminate the threat when Brandie's tone changed.

"You know, Zubict, I've never said I wouldn't help Rey," Brandie whispered. She and her captor had switched places. She was close enough to put her hands behind her and wave her fingers in his direction, as if she'd heard him close Toby's door. Then she flattened her palm in a signal to stop.

Mitch was inches from handing her a gun. Conversation ceased and the floor creaked. He knew which board from the couple of times he'd visited the Quinn house. Knew that his opponent was two feet from the hallway. And knew that something had alerted him that Mitch was there.

He grabbed Brandie's hand and pulled her into the hall, launching himself into the living room. He landed in Zubict's chest. The man's gun fired wildly.

Mitch caught the gun hand and squeezed until it dropped to the floor. Brandie stood in the hall, searching. He couldn't tell her to get to Toby. Talking would risk completely blowing his cover. Her parents would hear him.

"Brandie! What's happening?" yelled her mother.

"Untie me, Brandie," Bud said at the same instant.

Without his gun, Zubict darted for the door. Mitch had height and weight on the shorter man with fancy shoes. Those same pointy posh loafers slipped like a dog from a cartoon spinning in one place.

Mitch barreled into him from behind, tackling him to the floor. The little man let out a pathetic squeal. It might have been funny, but he'd held Brandie's family hostage and threatened Toby more than once.

He yanked the man's left hand behind his back. This really wasn't a fight at all. He raised himself to a knee and heard Zubict moan.

"What the hell's going on in there, Brandie?" Bud yelled from the kitchen.

Mitch looked up just in time to see a lamp crashing to

the top of his head. Flaming red hair swirled, cool blue nails held on to the base. It took a lot to bring him to his knees. Brandie had managed it twice in one day.

Chapter Five

The police had arrived, and Brandie's guilty conscience was working double time. She was the reason Mitch had not one, but two lumps on his head. The spiraling red-white-and-blue lights entertained Toby and a host of neighbors from a couple of blocks. Marfa was a small town and everyone knew what went on. But she was in the dark.

Something had been happening at her garage and she needed to get a clue. And it all hinged on Mitch's timely arrival. Four days after their mechanic of six years just disappeared, Mitch had driven up looking for work. It was also about the time the phone calls from Rey had started. Maybe *Mitch* was the connection to Rey King that she didn't know about.

When she'd quit school, she'd spoken to her former college advisor about what she could do. He'd implied that she might be able to help with a business venture. So it didn't take much imagination to conclude the reason he was interested now had something to do with drugs if he was involved.

The paramedics continued working on Mitch. Taking his pulse, attempting to revive him with smelling salts. She had to get closer and fill him in as soon as he woke up so their stories matched.

Or rather her lies.

Mitch attempted to sit up on the rolling stretcher. The paramedic lost the battle as he swung his legs over the side, rubbing his lumps. "Again?"

"Looks like your head came into contact with a lamp. A wrench this morning and a lamp tonight." Pete stood at Mitch's side, notepad in hand, bad look on his face.

"I think it's heroic how he tried to save me from those horrible men." She moved from behind Pete, took the cold pack from the paramedic and gently held it on top of Mitch's head.

"He doesn't seem to be very good at it," Pete said. "Your dad's sawed-off shotgun was a better weapon than Mitch's head."

Mitch's eyes narrowed. His wonderful lips compressed shut, the vein in his forehead was prominent so she let the cold pack slip a little. She took the opportunity to move in closer as Mitch's hand grabbed her wrist.

"What happened?" he asked through gritted teeth.

"Don't you remember, Mr. Striker?" Pete raised an eyebrow along with a corner of his mouth. Did he have the same suspicions as her? That Mitch was somehow involved with Rey's men?

"Brandie needed a ride. I got tired of waiting in the car. I went to the door. Then nothing. Did someone try to break in like at the shop?" It was a question, but his horrible attempt at sounding innocent made her stand straight. Pete faced him again instead of walking away.

"Just like at the garage." Pete wrote another note then put his pad away. "You're lucky they used a lamp instead of just shooting you. Any idea what they were looking for?"

"I just work at Junior's, Sheriff. How would I know?" The cold pack slipped again.

"Thanks, Brandie, I got this. Toby? Your mom?" he asked. His eyes spoke volumes. He was going along with her lies for some reason on his own agenda and she'd hear about it later. The grip on her wrist let her know that.

"They're fine. Toby curled into a basket and slept through the whole thing. It took a while to find him under the quilt squares."

"Don't worry, Mitch, I showed that SOB who tied us up what's what." Her father had grabbed the shotgun as soon as she'd untied him.

The sheriff was still much too close for Brandie to tell Mitch why she'd hit him.

"Bud nicked one with his shotgun. We found traces of blood on the porch." The sheriff crossed his arms and didn't seem in a hurry to head anywhere else.

"Pellets, not a real shell. But I yelled at him that a real bullet was waiting if he set foot inside our door again," her father bragged. "Damn. Now I have to replace the screen."

"Can I ask why no one here thought to call me until a shot was fired?" Pete asked.

"Olivia dialed 9-1-1 as soon as we got to the phone."

"Why didn't you use *your* cell phone?" Mitch asked her, turning his face up and letting the ice pack fall to the portable gurney.

She kept glancing at Pete who waited for her answer, pencil in hand, ready to make note of her answer. Should she tell him that she knew who had ordered his gunman to come and threaten her family?

"I think it's in the car."

"Any clue as to who these guys are, Sheriff?" Mitch asked after an outward sigh and slight shake of his head.

"Bud took off after the guy and got a partial plate," the sheriff explained. "Fool thing to do. But it's a start on catching them and finding out why the Quinns' place is being targeted."

"Did the men say anything to you, Bud, or give a reason?" Mitch asked from just behind her. "Did you get a look at any of them?"

"I only saw the backsides of those three when they took off. Ha." He slapped his knee, then slapped his hand in a loud clap. "The last stupid dope isn't from around these parts if he didn't think I already had a gun aimed at his privates."

Her dad was laughing about a man threatening his life. He seemed to have forgotten all about being tied up when she'd arrived.

"I'm so glad you're okay." She hugged her father, and he hugged quickly then set her away from his chest. But that was okay. The return hug was more than she'd expected. "Do you think they'll be back?"

"There's no way to tell why he chose your parents' home. Maybe it had something to do with the break-in at the garage this morning. Maybe not." Pete shrugged. "We may never know."

But she knew. Mitch knew. Even though he'd taken care of two of the men waiting in the car, they'd be back because Rey said they'd be back. They'd force her to cooperate by threatening her family. She'd been lucky this round. Just lucky.

Her mechanic would be extremely angry if he'd seen that she'd slammed him with the lamp. Maybe he hadn't, but she should explain anyway. If he'd followed the men, he probably would have caught them. And then where would she be? Tangled in another lie.

Whatever Rey wanted her to do. Whatever he wanted from the garage that he hadn't told her about. He hadn't found it and was angry that Mitch had sent him on his way tonight. He would definitely be back.

"Do you think the highway patrol will find them?"

"There's no telling, Bud. They may stay away." Pete

looked at Mitch with some hidden message one man shoots another. "I'd be afraid to face your good shooting."

Her dad began to laugh and leaned on the car near him. Mitch's car. He gave it a long glare, squinted his eyes at her and then Mitch. He must have finally realized they had arrived together. "Something wrong with your car, girl?"

"I—"

"Flat tire, sir. I'd already closed the station and offered to just bring her home." More lies and this time one her father wouldn't easily believe.

"See that's all you do."

"Got it." Mitch leaned closer, his breath a light warmth on her neck. "Right after we discuss who really hit me over the head," he whispered.

"Mind if we go, Sheriff? I want to get Toby to bed." She heard Mitch's harrumph behind her. He remembered the lamp and wasn't happy.

"Go ahead. If we need anything else, I know where you live. And Mr. Striker, don't think bad about our sleepy little town. Crime isn't the norm here."

"No plans to leave a good job, Sheriff."

Brandie hugged her father again, just because she could get away with it. One of the deputies was dusting for fingerprints so she led the way to the back door. Out of earshot, she did an about-face and poked Mitch in the chest.

"I do not like lying to my parents."

"I didn't much care for you lying to me this morning. Or lying to the sheriff about who hit me on the head. That might come back to bite you in your tush."

"You are definitely a cop. Go ahead and admit it. Anyone could tell by the way you moved in the house during that fight. Both of Zubict's men complained about you. They wanted to kill you. At least you don't work for them."

"Let's get Toby and go to a secure location." He turned

her by her shoulders and gently pushed hard enough to get her walking.

"Really? A secure location? What kind of talk is that for a noncop?" She stopped on the first porch step and faced him again. This time a little closer to his face. Too close not to notice his deep-set eyes that were the perfect shade of brown. "You don't think my house is safe?"

"Do you?"

She wanted to kiss him. To celebrate that they'd survived a hostage situation. She fisted her hands into the sides of her apron. Realizing she still had it on for a reason. A reason shaped like a gun.

"You've got a heck of a lot of nerve coming in here and trying to take over my life. I've taken care of myself for a long time and don't need your help." She verified they were alone and pulled his gun from under her apron where she'd stuffed it while her dad had scared Zubict away.

Mitch threw his hands in the air and took a step back. "You don't want my help, I can understand English. I'll wait in the car before you shoot me."

"Wait. Here. It's yours. I didn't think you wanted Zubict to take another one from you." She handed him his weapon, and he stuffed it under his shirt in his waistband. "Do you think they'll come back or might already be at my house waiting?"

"It's a strong possibility. King has threatened you and your son twice. I'm taking him seriously. I just need an hour for you to hear me out."

"Okay. I know I owe you an explanation for this morning, but nothing more." He rubbed the knot closer to his forehead. "Right, I need to explain why I hit you tonight, too. But my life is my own and whatever agency you work for—since you say you aren't a cop—you need to remember that my past stays *my* past."

"DON'T YOU THINK we should call Cord and Kate before we just drop in?" Brandie asked from beside him.

"It's not too late and I don't think they'll mind. I'd rather not use the phone." He pushed the gas, speeding down the highway whether another car was in sight or not.

"I hit you with the lamp, but you already know that. You couldn't see the gun. They looked so mad, I thought it was the only way to get everyone out of there alive."

Mitch was still digesting her declaration of her past staying hers. What could she have done that was so terrible she didn't want it mentioned? Hell, he was still digesting the fact that she'd hit him over the head to save him from being shot.

"Telling me there was a gun to my head might have been easier."

"I didn't think you'd listen." She twisted in the seat to face him and placed her hand on his upper arm. "Look, Toby's asleep and I'd rather not walk in on the McCreas blind. Care to start talking? And start by telling me why I need to stay overnight out in the boonies."

"I need two answers first," he said, fingers tapping on the console between them.

"Okay."

"Why should I trust you? For all I know you're working for Rey."

It was hard to judge her reaction. She was so full of contradictions. Her words and actions did not support the woman he'd known as the café manager.

"Fair question. I'm not working for him. I don't know who he is."

"That's not an answer and I'll just keep my information to myself." She crossed her arms and looked at the window away from him.

He could see a wall going up between them. She'd slap

down the mortar and he'd throw on another brick. It was up so fast and strong that unless he took drastic measures, it would be permanent.

"Okay, okay. What I'm about to tell you can't be shared—" Cord would kill him.

"If you aren't a cop, then you're a Ranger. Right? That's why you're taking me to the home of a Texas Ranger?" She was too smart for her own good.

"Hey, if you knew, then why the drama?"

"I didn't know for certain, but it's better that I guessed, isn't it? I mean, now you won't be lying when you tell Cord you didn't tell me."

Brandic was completely at ease. No signs of stress. It was like they were out for a Sunday picnic and heading back to town.

"So you were awake this morning," she continued. "No wonder you wanted to spend time with me. Either you think I'm working with Rey King or you feel responsible for our safety."

"It wasn't like that at all." It had never been, even when he told Cord it would be kept professional. A small part of him had been looking for an excuse to twirl her around the jukebox. A big part of him had been wanting to kiss her from day two.

"At all?"

He normally could have shrugged it off. He'd done it hundreds of times. He was pretty good with nonverbal communication. But this time, his face held on to the lie he'd told Cord.

"That's what I thought." She crossed her arms, holding tight to her sides.

He couldn't straighten her out. Not only was it his career, but if she knew he was deeply attracted to her she might forget. A little mistake could get her killed. "What was the second thing you needed to know?"

"It doesn't matter. You're just doing your duty."

"Man alive." He felt like cursing at how she could get to conclusions he was trying to hide. "If I were just doing my job, I wouldn't have blown my cover on the very afternoon I got a lecture about blowing my damn cover."

They rolled to a stop outside the McCreas' house.

"Maybe I should have left you with your parents. I think your dad has a handle on protecting his home."

The porch light flipped on, and Cord slowly came through the screen door, dressed only in his jeans and sidearm.

"Then why did you bring me here and admit you're undercover?"

"Basically, I want you to disappear. Stay someplace safe, away from Marfa or Presidio County. King is out for blood and it's too damn dangerous for you to stay working in the café."

"Mitch?" Cord used a knuckle to tap on the window, waiting for it to be cranked down. "This better be good."

"It is, sir."

"Were you followed?"

"Not to my knowledge, and I turned Brandie's phone off."

"When did you do that?"

"Car seat fiasco. Who knew moving a car seat from one vehicle to the next took three adults?" Mitch couldn't look Cord in the eye. He was disobeying a direct order, several by coming here.

"I did. Enough times that I bought a second car seat. You better come inside. Need any help?" Cord turned back to his porch after Mitch shook his head.

"I'm not going anywhere." Brandie crossed her arms

and flattened her lips into a straight, determined line. "I have a home and I have a business to run. You guys can't force me to leave."

"Are you willing to sacrifice your family for the café?"

"That's not a fair question. Of course, I don't want anything bad to happen to them. But the café's the only living I have. If I leave there's no telling what will happen to business. Surely there's another way?"

"There is and I'm certain my superiors are going to ask it of you. I want you to refuse. It's not safe…for either of you." How could he get her to understand?

"We should get inside. Your real boss is waiting at the door."

Mitch reached out, securing her hand in his until she looked at him. "I'm deadly serious. It's too dangerous."

"I made a mistake several years ago and have worried ever since that secret would destroy my life. I hate that feeling as much as seeing everything I've worked for being taken away from me." She wiped a fast falling tear off her cheek with the back of her knuckle. "I'm staying here. You should go inside and talk things over with Cord. He looked pretty upset."

"Whatever you did—"

He left the rest of the words unsaid. She didn't know him. He had no way to convince her of anything. He had no proof that King had any connection with the Mexican drug cartel or the gunrunning into Mexico. He just felt it down deep. Maybe because he'd watched her for the past six months and this was the first lead they'd had.

No logical road to deduction, just a gut feeling. Not the most intelligent way to convince the Texas Rangers.

Chapter Six

Mitch dreaded the earful he was about to receive from Cord who could report back to his captain at any time. But there was no denying that he deserved it. He'd let down his guard and blown his cover with his prime suspect.

Now a suspect—at least according to the Rangers. He still didn't believe it.

"You know about our fight with the Mexican gangs. Do you think the men trying to hurt Brandie's family are their associates?"

Cord and his wife, Kate, had a history with the people King worked for. Even a closemouthed mechanic heard the stories how the couple fought off one of their vindictive leaders. Maybe they could do a better job of explaining the gravity of the danger to Brandie.

"How long have you known that I work with your husband?" Mitch asked Kate, avoiding her question.

"You just told me this minute." She laughed. "Cord said repeatedly that there was something off about the mechanic at Junior's. That's how he explains all your private conversations at the garage. I'll never trust him again." She smiled at her husband as he came in from the kitchen. "I can't believe he kept the secret."

"You'll have to excuse us, Kate." Cord had two beers, handing one to Mitch.

"I can help get Toby inside if you guys want to talk in Cord's study." Kate pointed to a door on the opposite side of the house.

"If you can get Brandie out of the car." Mitch didn't think he'd have any luck doing it. That was one of the reasons he'd come in alone. "She needs a little convincing."

Cord led the way to his study, shaking his head, scratching his chin. Once inside, he closed the door. The only window in the room didn't open to the front of the house so it didn't matter that the wooden blinds were tilted to where Mitch couldn't see out.

"She'll be okay. You can hear a car coming for half a mile at this time of night." Cord sat. "So you blew your cover."

"Yes, sir."

"I'm a Ranger, just like you. My name, you know it? Use it. Don't start *sirring* me when you're in trouble." He tipped the bottle to his lips, not looking like a superior about to give someone the ax.

"My captain at Border Security Operations is a little more strict."

"Bet you don't come to his house at midnight, either. It's okay, I appreciate that they loaned you to the task force. But I told you this morning the situation with Brandie wouldn't end well. You're too involved."

Mitch hadn't been invited to sit down. Manners or nerves let him take advantage and walk the perimeter of the room. Listening for signs that Kate had coaxed Brandie inside.

"You warned me about Toby. I'm keeping that in mind. Circumstances have changed. She was threatened."

"I believe you mentioned that this afternoon."

"A man from Alpine, Rey King, paid us a visit after we closed. He threatened her family."

"She's working with King?" He sat forward.

"No. I don't think she's working with anyone. Do you know about this guy? Who is he?"

Cord tossed a folder his way. Just glancing through it, Mitch could tell the Rangers had been keeping tabs on King awhile. He had ties to more than just the south side of the border. "Chicago, New York, Philly…why isn't the DEA more involved in this operation?"

"They've been kept up-to-date and are waiting on evidence. No one's talking and we can't prove a thing. If you think Brandie may know something—"

"I don't."

"But you seem certain she needs protection. That doesn't justify that you've blown your cover."

"I didn't have much of a choice. Okay, I did. You're right. But when Brandie accused me of working for King I saw her shutting me out, and we need her. I know she has valuable information. I just don't know what it is. Maybe you can talk some sense into her about going back to the café— It's too dangerous for her and Toby to—"

"Ever have this happen before, Mitch?"

The front door closed, but he didn't hear the kid or noises in the other room. Was Brandie really going to just sit in the car until he pulled her out kicking and screaming? He would. She needed to be protected from her pride.

"Have what happen?"

"Do you make it a habit of getting seriously involved with your suspect when you're undercover?"

Cord's accusation faded with the sound of an old engine purring to life.

"What the hell?" Mitch banged the beer bottle down on the desk and shoved his hand into his empty pocket.

"Nothing personal, you know I have to ask."

"No way." He pulled open the office door and heard tires spitting up gravel and turned back to face Cord. "She's stealing my car."

TOBY WAS TUCKED in his bed and still sound asleep. It took Mitch longer to get to her house than she'd thought. She would have cleaned up or even gotten her shower out of the way if she'd known it would take that long. When the car pulled away, she realized Cord had dropped him off and Mitch would need his keys.

Surprisingly, he didn't bang on the front door and he didn't try to burst inside. He stood on her porch stoop for a couple of minutes, pinching the bridge of his nose as if he had a headache. She opened the door before he moved again.

"What do you want, Mitch? Besides your car." She tossed him his keys and crossed her arms, waiting for his rant.

His lips flattened as he shoved the rabbit's foot and two keys into his pocket. He had a very simple life living in the garage's back room. "Two keys. One to my garage and one to your car. I don't suppose you have some in storage somewhere? Some other home that you'll go to when this is over?"

She was angrier than she'd thought she'd been when she took his car and sped back from Valentine all alone. Always alone. She should know and be used to that frame of mind by now.

"I'm not leaving town and my job. I'm not staying out at the McCreas' place," she said for emphasis.

"I realize that," he said softly, acting sort of withdrawn or reverting to his short-sentenced mechanic routine.

"I also won't tell anyone who you really are—as if I actually know."

"I really am Mitch Striker."

"Oh." She took a step back inside the house, her anger deflated by the sorrowful look in the brown eyes staring at her. "Well, it's been a long day, I should get some sleep."

"Agreed." He sat on the porch, leaning back against the vinyl siding.

"I said I'm hitting the hay. See you tomorrow." Brandie had to go farther on the porch to look at his face.

"Understood." His head was leaning next to the front window, his eyes closed.

She plopped down next to him. "What are you doing?"

"Making a statement."

"To me? It's not necessary." And yet, her heart did a little flip-flop in her chest, excited that he'd sit on her porch to do so. "No one's sitting across the street ready to break in and tie me to a chair. Zubict did that to make his own statement. So there aren't any threats."

"Damn straight. Not while I'm here. You should go inside." He hadn't looked at her, completely at ease leaning back and staking his territory.

She stood, feeling like she was talking to her son. "Okay then."

She shouldn't ask him inside. It would be all over town. Her dad would find out. But couldn't she explain that he'd been worried about her? It was the truth, after all.

She saw the curtains next door be pulled back and dropped quickly back into place. Her neighbors were already paying too much attention to her. "Good grief, Mitch. You can't sleep out here on my porch."

"I agree. I'll get a nap back at the garage tomorrow." He shifted uncomfortably on the cement porch.

"You can't stay here all night. People will talk. Marfa's a real small town. They don't overlook things like this."

He opened his eyes, zeroing in on hers, catching her to him without a touch. "I'm not leaving you alone."

"Come inside." She cleared her throat that had become all warm, making her voice like syrup. A little stronger she said, "You can stay on the couch, but don't get any ideas."

"None that weren't already there."

She gasped. That was the word that specifically described what her mouth did with the air she almost choked on.

"New or old," she coughed out. "Nothing's going to happen."

"Tonight." He nodded once. "I agree."

"Ever. Not ever." She marched to the hall closet, completely off-kilter and much too warm after Mitch's brazen statements. She had to squash the idea. She couldn't get involved with anyone, especially a cool Texas Ranger who had been lying to her for six months. He wasn't who she thought he was. She grabbed sheets and a blanket for the couch.

"I don't have any extra pillows so the couch cushion will have—" He wasn't in the living room. She poked her head into her small kitchen that was still empty. "Mitch?" Turning around he was directly behind her. "Oh. Wow. You scared me."

"Just checking the windows to make sure everything's locked and secure." He took the linens. "You ready to explain to me what's going on with King?"

Could she trust him? She was in this mess because she'd trusted the wrong person. And if she explained one part of her problem, she'd have to explain the other. And if that came out, she'd be out on her ear. Everything she had been working for would be gone.

Toby would be homeless.

"I take that look to mean no. Might as well get some

shut-eye, then. It's been a long day and I have a lot of catching up to do at the garage tomorrow."

"That's it? No interrogation or coaxing my secrets from me?"

He tossed the sheets on the chair nearest him and did an about-face. "I could live with some coaxing." He waggled his eyebrows. "You want me to…coax your secrets?"

She laughed at his silliness and felt her body blushing at his suggestiveness. "I was thinking more along the lines of thumbscrews."

"Naw, we gave that up in the last century."

She was so confused. He wasn't upset and yelling at her that she'd taken his car? Or arguing about staying in Marfa. He had plans to work tomorrow and was content to sleep on her couch. She did feel safer and she'd probably sleep sounder knowing anyone was in the next room.

Who was she fooling? She felt better because it would be Mitch on her couch.

"Okay, so, my bedroom's on the right."

"I know." He smiled by tilting up the sexy corner of his mouth and winking.

"Sure, you'd know that because…ah…"

Whoa. The image that popped into her mind wasn't of him sleeping on the couch alone. And it was no longer of her sleeping in her bed all alone, either. *Oh, my*.

"Because Toby's door has his favorite superheroes taped on it."

His T-shirt came off over his head, and this time she counted the defined and rigid abs. He sat and pulled his boots off. "'Night, Brandie."

She didn't—couldn't—look at him any longer. She was slowly closing her door and heard Mitch on the phone with someone. She used the lock for the very first time, keeping her mysterious mechanic out and her nosy curiosity in. She wasn't about to eavesdrop on his conversation. She had enough secrets to keep.

The T-shirt she'd borrowed from him during the morning embarrassment was still on her pillow. She changed into it just because she could and got under the covers. She inhaled deeply, loving Mitch's male scent as she drifted into dreamland.

Chapter Seven

Little fingers pried at his eyelids. Mitch had peeked at Toby a couple of minutes earlier, as the little boy had poked at Mitch's puffed-up cheek to get him to make a popping sound with his lips.

It was still early, still dark. He hadn't slept much. The couch was too short and his mind too uneasy. First with the threats from King and his men. Then the accusations Cord had made about his personal life.

It was a revelation to Mitch that he had a personal life at all. Popping the air from his cheeks was a game he and Toby played often. The kid had been excited to find him on the couch, but not freaked out. Mitch expected Brandie to come in at any minute and tell him he needed to leave.

Funny thing was, he didn't want to leave. He was fine keeping Toby occupied and letting his mom get some extra sleep. He let the little fingers poke his air-puffed cheeks one more time, made the noise the kid loved and popped his eyes open at the same time.

Toby jumped and giggled. A sweet sound Mitch never got tired of.

So he was involved. So what? It reminded him what he was undercover for. He was protecting women and children like this family from the threats of men like Rey King. There wasn't anything wrong with that.

To which Cord had replied there was if it interfered. So was it?

Mitch tickled Toby, who squirmed on the beige-carpeted floor. "You ready to eat, kid?"

"Scrambled eggs?"

"Sure, I can do that."

"I'll get mom."

He took off, but Mitch's arm got him around the middle. His little feet kept running like a cartoon and his giggle filled the room. Another trick they did when Toby visited the café and he was running when he should be walking.

Cord had warned him to hang in the background, to let the situation with King happen without interference or rushing in to save the day.

Maybe he was ready to let those close to him know he could save the day. It just seemed like he smiled a lot more in Marfa—at least when people couldn't see him.

He had the eggs scrambled in the bowl and the pan hot when Brandie wandered into the kitchen.

"Morning."

"Nice shirt." He noticed his T-shirt and the blush that crept up the fair redhead's neck and cheeks. She crossed her arms and did a one-eighty from the room.

Mitch had also noticed her pert nipples and her long curls messed up like she'd had a restless sleep, too. He cooked Toby's eggs, gave him chocolate milk and buttered toast, then sat at the table with him.

"Mitch?"

"Yup, that's me."

"Are you gonna live here now? 'Cause if you did, we could get bunk beds and share my room." Toby was all eyes and seriousness, milk-stained lip and all.

Mitch didn't have the heart to tell him it wasn't a possibility. Then again, what was stopping him? He remembered the way his T-shirt had looked on Brandie earlier. Sharing a room with someone wasn't such an unpleasant idea.

"Eat up, kid. We'll talk about those bunks later."

He was scooping the last bite of eggs in his mouth when Brandie emerged. Her plate had grown cold before she returned completely dressed and ready for another day at the café.

She put the eggs between two pieces of bread and wrapped it in a napkin. "I laid out your clothes, buddy. Go brush your teeth and get dressed."

"Does Mitch have to brush his teeth?"

"Sure I do, kid. But mine's at the garage."

"You need one here then, 'cause you gotta brush before you leave the house." Toby pushed in his chair and scampered from the room.

"You shouldn't encourage him," she said while washing up his mess.

"I was going to do that."

"It's okay. You cooked, I'll clean." She stretched on her tiptoes to peek out the high window over the sink. "Better get your boots on. Mrs. Escalon's on her way over to stay with Toby. I have no idea how I'm going to explain this. Maybe you can leave without her seeing your car."

"How about the truth. I stayed here because of the attack on your family. And your car's at the café. Remember?"

"I'm afraid you staying here will be gossipier news than my dad filling an intruder's behind with buckshot." She dried the pan, looking away again.

He didn't know what to say. He'd put her in a compromising situation. His first thought was that he didn't care. It had been the right thing to do. Then again...he cared. Enough to blow his cover and tell her the truth about himself. Something he'd never thought of doing before.

"I KNEW I HAD some catching up to do in the garage." Mitch pushed hard to get the door open. "But this?"

Supplies were everywhere. Shelves had been overturned. Invoices, estimates and receipts out of their file folders and on every surface.

"Why didn't the alarm go off? I thought you said the sheriff would have extra patrols?" Brandie said right behind him.

He'd had a great morning, sharing a homemade breakfast with the kid who had been superexcited to see him. Until a reminder that the real world would see his staying overnight as wrong. Then a phone call from Brandie's dad had shifted all the good to bad. Mitch heard him yelling through the cell about a certain car parked all night in her driveway.

He hadn't set the alarm. "I think we were in too big of a hurry last night and left without turning the blasted thing on."

"You're right. All I did was lock the door." She scooted paperwork out of her path with her toe. She looked up to see the vandalism to his immaculate garage. "Would you like me to call Ricky in to help you clean this mess up?"

"I'll take care of it after the sheriff finishes."

"We're not calling Pete."

He spun around, letting her walk into his chest. He secured her balance and quickly dropped his hands because in spite of all the distraction, he was still thinking about her in his T-shirt. "Why not? What are you afraid of them finding?"

"We already know who did this. There's no reason to bring the sheriff's department into it. It's not like I'm going to tell them anything." She pointed a finger at him. "You can't, either."

"No, we don't. I know you've been threatened by King.

Your family's been threatened. And now you've been robbed. I also know you're too frightened to go to the police."

"I'm not afraid, Mitch. I'm angry." She dug her phone out of the piece of luggage she called a purse, scrolled and dialed. "There's a huge difference."

She passed through the garage to the café, growling as she tripped on a ratchet extension and slid in some spilled brake fluid. Mitch followed, picking up Jacob's radiator replacement hose that he'd been waiting a week to arrive. He didn't have time to think about garage customers and yet he was.

"Hand him the phone, Zubict. I want to talk with Rey." She waited at the café entrance, not moving into the room.

He could see over her head and it wasn't a pretty sight. Everything was trashed. He heard a sniff, saw her fingers swipe away a tear. Then he saw the irreplaceable jukebox…smashed, the records thrown around the room, destroyed.

He thought he'd been mad seeing the garage. This was senseless and clearly a threat. The cost of repairs and replacing everyday items they needed for the café would be astronomical.

"I'd like to listen." He stood behind her while she pressed Speaker without asking why or telling him to mind his own business. He wanted her to bury her face in his chest so he could comfort her completely. Instead, he stiffly put his hand on her sweater-covered shoulder.

Mitch had given his word to Cord that nothing was going on between him and Brandie. The teasing last night had been fun, but that's all it was. The needless destruction hit him deep in a place he didn't know he had. He wanted to find Rey King and rip his head to shreds.

"*Hola*, baby."

"I hope you found whatever you were looking for," she demanded. "But you went too far tearing my place apart."

"You know we didn't find it, Brandie. Moving the package somewhere else won't help you. We'll get everything back. But this is your last warning, sweetheart. Give us what we want or someone's going to pay the price. Might even be that new boyfriend of yours. Thanks for getting him out of there so we could have a looksee."

"I didn't—"

"You're forgetting our agreement. You return my property or your parents will be in for a shock."

King disconnected. Mitch nudged Brandie forward into the room, flipped over a chair that was still intact and made her sit. He took another of the old-fashioned café chairs and straddled it so they were facing each other.

"You ready to tell me what's going on now?" he asked.

Tears filled her when she looked up at him. "The staff will be here in a few minutes."

"We tell them to come back after the sheriff has processed the scene."

"But—" She swiped at another tear. "Fine. It'll look weird if I don't let them."

"More than weird, Brandie. At the moment you're connected with a known criminal organization."

She shook her head. "Rey King is an Alpine college professor in the Spanish Department. He's got his mind set that my former mechanic hid something of his here."

"Like what? Money? Drugs?"

"At first I thought he was kidding around. But then I assumed Glen had been selling weed. I didn't realize that he even knew Rey."

"And you haven't moved anything from the garage? Did King get in touch with you after Glen disappeared?"

"You mean after he left. You found a note in the desk, remember? Was that a lie, too?"

"Look, Brandie, you have to remember that I've been undercover. I wasn't allowed to tell anyone why."

"Just how long have you been lying to everyone you know, playing Mitch the Mechanic?"

He recognized that she needed a place to vent her anger at the situation as much as she was hurt by finding out he'd been lying to her. They needed to stay focused on one problem at a time. Right now, it was her problem with King.

"We don't have time for my life story. I need you to tell me how you know Rey King and why he has control over you."

"I can't trust you with that."

"Brandie, you either trust me or you spill it to the Texas Rangers' captain who will be showing up when you're arrested for obstructing justice. It's that simple. I've already been told I don't have much time."

She jumped up. "You're leaving?"

He'd just threatened to arrest her and she asked if he was leaving. At any other time, he might think that was a good sign. Hell, it was a good sign.

"I've already been here too long." He tugged her to the office chair. "But the main thing is that the Rangers think they have enough for a real investigation. We need solid connections to bring in the DEA or more Rangers."

"About me? I haven't done anything. Why would they want to look into my life?"

That was the second time she'd flinched about her past. This was about Rey King. He needed anything she'd spill. "You've got to give me something to hold them off."

"I...can't."

The pain in her eyes was genuine. It wrenched his heart and his gut, but he pulled his phone out and got in touch with Cord. "Yeah, another break-in. They smashed the place up pretty good."

"Do you know what they're looking for?"

"She won't tell me." Mitch looked at a fiery redhead determined to keep her secrets.

"Something's not adding up. You said she was angry at King. I just have a hard time thinking that she'd be in business with him. What about the former mechanic? Think he was the problem?"

"Didn't everyone have a hard time believing the last informant you found who worked with Bishop? What about the one who worked with Rook?"

"I'm not an informant," Brandie said with a huff. "Rey wrecked the place because I'm *not* telling him anything."

"I get it," Cord stated in his ear. "Brandie's listening to your side of the conversation and you're trying to scare her into telling you? I can tell you that the only people I've seen scare her are the Quinns themselves."

"So you think I should talk with her parents?"

"Don't go there, Mitch," Brandie said softly.

"Good advice. You might need to run interference with the locals." He disconnected and called the sheriff's department, reporting the break-in.

"From what I can tell, you have less than ten minutes to convince me." He hated threatening her. Hated it.

Once Cord heard that Rey King was involved, he explained that he was a new major player in gun running across the border. All law enforcement agencies were under pressure to take this guy off the streets.

"Are you a man of your word, Mitch? Are you trustworthy?"

He took her soft, shaking hand in his. He was the person responsible for the uncontrollable tremor. King had destroyed her place and she'd grown angry. It was his threat of talking to her parents that made her tremble. His threat.

"You don't have any reason to trust me, Brandie. But I swear to you, I want to help. I want to get you out of this mess. But I can't unless I know what's going on. You have to tell me."

"This—" she pointed to her wedding ring "—is my mother's. I've never really been married."

"I don't understand. Isn't there a picture of you with your deceased husband at your parents' house? What about Toby?"

"The picture is really Toby's dad, but we were never married. My parents were embarrassed that I went away to school and came home pregnant. I had nowhere else to go." Her hands twisted in the edge of her shirt. Tears fell down her cheeks.

He couldn't imagine being alone and going through something like that. "What, were you eighteen?"

She nodded. At eighteen, he'd been a senior in high school, stealing beer and partying 'til dawn. One thing his dad had been blunt with him about was using protection to prevent early fatherhood.

"What about Toby's dad? I haven't seen anyone around in six months, so I assume he's not in the picture? Does he know?"

"My dad said I couldn't live here, that it would shame them with the community. So my mother came up with the story that I married a man in the Army, he shipped out and was killed in action. So, you see, I'm a liar, too."

She hadn't answered his question about the father.

"He should know people don't think that way about unwed mothers anymore."

"Don't you see? It didn't matter what people would

really think. It only mattered what my dad thought they were thinking. In his eyes, his friends pity me now."

Mitch had heard Bud talking about Toby's war hero father more than once. He told the story like it really happened. "King thinks you have his property and is going to expose your secret if you don't give it back. How does King know?"

"He was my advisor in college."

Their attention was drawn to the garage door before he could ask more details. Great, not a deputy. It was the sheriff himself. Again. The man was always on duty.

"Anybody here?"

"We're in the café." Mitch dreaded another confrontation. In fact, being the town drifter and the first place the police looked for answers after trouble happened was getting sort of old.

"So Pete doesn't know you're undercover?" she whispered.

"It's better that way."

"Funny meeting you here again, Striker." The sheriff leaned against the door frame. "I'd say good morning, but I don't think that would be accurate."

"You work a lot of hours, Sheriff. Late last night, early this morning. You must be exhausted." Mitch looked at his watch, wondering how soon he could call Cord. "Looks like they came in the back garage window."

There was no way he'd share all of the story. His captain would kill him if he didn't give over all the details. It wouldn't change how they went after King, but if it got out, it would really destroy Brandie.

"My dispatchers have been instructed to call me whenever there's a problem concerning you." Pete started to push his fingers through his hair but stopped before they got caught in his hair gel. "I saw the broken glass. The extra patrols I had by here last night didn't see a thing. Any working theories?"

"Sure," Brandie answered before Mitch could take a deep breath. "They didn't find what they wanted yesterday morning, so they tied my parents up as a distraction last night and came back while all your deputies were on our lawn?"

"Makes sense. It would be a reason why they harassed your parents." He walked around along the wall to the jukebox. "Now that's a downright shame. That smash looks like someone was angry. Any idea what they were looking for?"

"Not a clue," Mitch answered quickly. The look of relief he received from Brandie was worth all the ear chewing he'd receive from his captain.

Chapter Eight

"Mind if I take a look around, Brandie?" Pete asked, seeming to look at whatever he wanted anyway. "I'll need a list of anything that's missing. Hardy will be here to take pictures and document the damage for insurance. His shift starts at seven."

"Thanks, and go right ahead. It all looks the same, though."

"Have you told Bud yet?" he asked as he sifted through chairs toward the garage.

No two ways about it, her parents were going to freak. How would she break the news?

Mitch steadied her shoulders again and said, "You were the first call today. Surprised they aren't here already considering your 9-1-1 gossip line."

"Mitch, can you help me look at the storage room?" She had to get them away from each other. She gave a tug on his arm. Once in the back room she went to the wall and they cleared the shelf in front of the safe. "I bet you'd be best buds if he knew you were a Ranger."

"I doubt that. I haven't been a fan of small-town cops for the past two years. They've had every right to distrust a drifter like me."

"Is that how long you've been undercover?"

"You know I shouldn't answer that, Brandie." He

politely turned his back as he did every time he watched
her put the money in the safe.

"Thank goodness. Two days' proceeds still here."

"That doesn't make sense. I mean, I'm glad it is, but
why wouldn't they think you were keeping the stash in the
most secure place you have?" he whispered. "Unless…"

"Unless what? I told you I have no idea what Rey is
even looking for."

"Whatever it is, it won't fit in your safe."

"Mitch?" Pete called from just outside the door.

"That's great. Just great. I recognize that tone. I should
have checked my gear before calling him. Damn it." Mitch
squeezed his forehead. "Whatever happens, don't call
Cord. Promise me."

"What? Why?" Brandie was completely confused as
she watched Mitch put his hands up and back out of the
storage room.

"You know the routine. Lock your fingers behind your
neck and drop to your knees. Mitch Striker, you're under
arrest for the illegal possession of a firearm and illegal
substances with the intent to sale."

"Great." Pete hooked handcuffs on Mitch's right wrist.

"Tell him," she mouthed when Pete's face was turned.
"Tell him who you are."

Mitch kept his lips pressed together tightly, wincing as
his second arm was jerked behind his back.

"Hey, take it easy. This is all a mistake." She tried to
make Pete see reason.

"The mistake is that I gave this guy a chance to begin
with. There's something off about him, Brandie."

"You've got this all wrong. He's—"

"Don't argue with the sheriff." Mitch glared at her,
shaking his head.

Pete lifted Mitch's arms backward. "Up. Come on."

"Are you really arresting him? Everybody owns a gun in this town." Should she go against what Mitch said and stop him from being arrested?

"Brandie, go home and get Toby. Keep him with you until I'm back. Go to your dad's."

"Why do you think she needs protection?" Pete asked, being none too gentle with his prisoner.

"I'm not going anywhere. I have to clean up this mess."

Mitch jerked Pete to a stop, causing her mechanic to hiss a little in pain.

"You need to get to Toby. Don't you see why they've done this?"

"Stop talking. Sorry, Brandie, but this is a crime scene and you'll need to hold off cleaning while we process everything."

"How long will that take?"

"At least today. Just depends."

"Oh, good gravy. I don't know why you're doing this. Mitch doesn't use drugs." She followed them through the garage office entrance. "They came in here and planted that stuff."

Pete shook his head. "Regardless, I have to arrest him. Let's go."

"Wait," Mitch said. "Take the sedan home, I haven't checked your car. Will you let her take my car? I'll save you the trouble of a warrant. Check it out. It's not locked."

"I can't let her do that."

"Come on, Sheriff. She needs that car."

A deputy pulled up in a second Tahoe. Pete put Mitch in his truck where the window was already cracked.

"Mitch, you're scaring me." She kept her voice low while Pete spoke to Deputy Hardy.

"They set me up, Brandie. They want me out of the way

for some reason. Be overly cautious and spend the day at your mom and dad's with the shotgun."

"Will Cord get you out?"

"Someone from headquarters will let him know. I don't know who will post bail. They've invested a lot in this cover. That's how it normally works. Not my decision. Stay safe."

Pete climbed into his truck. "Hardy's going to watch the place. You good driving home? If you're worried about your car, I can drop you or have another deputy stop by to drive you wherever you need."

"I'll be okay." She looked at Mitch through the back window. The look she'd seen on his handsome face was back. Concerned, worried, analyzing…brows drawn into a straight line, he'd looked like that for most of the six months he'd been here. Yesterday had been different. She liked the man from yesterday and had really enjoyed breakfast this morning.

As soon as Pete was out of sight, her father drove up. He got out of his car, took one look at her tires—none of them flat—harrumphed loudly and started toward the café.

"Sorry, Mr. Quinn, um, this is a crime scene and we have to wait for the sheriff to get back."

"Nonsense, I own this place and you can't keep me out."

The deputy stepped in front of the door. "Sorry, sir, but I have to."

"It's a real mess inside, Dad, and there's nothing we can do today. Will you take me home? Toby's waiting."

He nodded grumpily. "Something wrong with your car?"

"Mitch thinks it's better if I don't drive it 'til he has a look."

"That drifter's taking on a lot of responsibility around

here." Her father didn't hint at animosity. It dripped from every word.

"Drifter? I thought you liked Mitch." She was a little confused at her father's hostility until she remembered that Mitch's car had been at her house all night. Her father had probably already had an earful of questions from her neighbors. Some about yesterday's break-in at the shop, lots about how he'd rescued everyone last night with his shotgun.

Fending off questions of why Mitch had been at her house had taken him off guard. In the five years she'd been back after dropping out of college, no one had ever stayed at the house she rented from her father.

"I like him fine as the hired help. He's a drifter. I expect him to move on any day. Maybe we should advertise for another mechanic."

"Why would we do that if he's good at his job? None of this is his fault. He stayed to make sure we were all right last night."

"I could have done that if you thought it was necessary. And if he's the hero in all this, then why did they arrest him?"

"It's all a mistake." She couldn't tell him Mitch had been framed by Rey King. That would lead to a host of other questions she wasn't prepared to discuss at the moment.

"I don't know why you hired him without a criminal background check."

She had taken care of verifying everything about Mitch Striker. Her dad was going to argue with her no matter what she answered. It was more important to consider what Mitch said. Why wouldn't he want her to call Cord? Because if he showed up then Pete would wonder what was so special about Mitch.

Stay with Toby, he'd said.

"Oh, my gosh, he thinks Toby is in danger." Chills rippled down her back and across her body. "Something's wrong, Daddy. I've got to get home."

Chapter Nine

"I hate small hick towns. The door was unlocked like I said. Good." Rey King directed his men through the hands-free mic on his cell. "The cops took the mechanic so she's on her way home. Stay on the phone and stay ready."

He and his men had been in Marfa all night—ransacking and watching. If the mechanic hadn't slept over at Brandie's, Rey would be at his home with Patrice having breakfast and...other things. He was stiff from sitting in the car. Each time he'd caught some sleep at that run-down café, one of his men would wake him with the news they hadn't found anything. He'd thrown a chair into the jukebox during his last frustrated rage.

A car pulled up and parked in the driveway of Brandie's house. She ran to the front door. Before her father was out of the car, she stood on the porch with her son in her arms. They waved, and the old man returned behind the wheel of his faded Buick and drove away. An old lady joined Brandie, blew kisses at the boy and took the steps carefully back to the house two doors down.

"Five minutes for Brandie to get relaxed and we go inside. She must know where the package is. The only person that hurts her is me. I am not losing everything because of this bitch or because one of you gets trigger-happy."

Rey adjusted his suit along with the new gun holster as

he got out of the car. He loved the feel of the holster and secretly practiced drawing his new Glock 21 .45 ACP. He liked the sound of the name and firepower of the bigger caliber.

It was a shame he couldn't use it today, but it had been easier to get the mechanic thrown in jail instead of confronting him. Drug charges were taken seriously in this little town.

Brandie came to the door at his knock. She was smart enough to keep it closed. Her son looked like he was still on her hip. His eyes were wide and as bright blue as hers. Most people would think he looked like his mother, but Rey could easily see the resemblance to his father.

"Come on, Brandie. Open up. We need to talk."

"I can hear you just fine." She twisted the dead bolt in an attempt to keep him outside.

"What? I'm not sure what you're saying." He lowered his voice and put his hand to his ear. He could see the ruse wasn't working. No sane person would open the door to a threat.

"It'll go better for you if you open up voluntarily," he said in his regular tone.

"When did you start acting like a gangster? You were my history professor and advisor. I can't believe I shared anything about my life with you."

"I still teach, Brandie. You know that." Then, just loud enough for his hands-free, he gave the go-ahead to break in the back door. "Now."

"I don't know what you want. I don't have anything of yours. So go away and leave us alone before I call the sheriff."

"We both know you won't do that. And why." Rey tugged on the bottom of his jacket again. The bigger gun definitely made the jacket more snug. He watched the neighborhood for signs that someone had noticed him walking there or that they heard the muffled screams inside the house. The dead bolt turned again and the door pulled open.

No drapes moved across the street and no sounds escaped from Brandie as he shuffled into the living room.

"How do you live like this?" he asked, not expecting an answer. "This reminds me of the place my mother rented when I was young like your boy. I do prefer the home I have her in now."

The little boy hadn't started crying yet. Although, he looked like his lungs were about to explode in Zubict's arms. Brandie's mouth had been quickly taped shut as he'd instructed. Zubict's partner had her arms pinned behind her back. She spoke volumes to her son through her expressive eyes.

"Let's be clear. You stay quiet and nothing happens to either of you. Nod if you understand." He waited for the reluctant agreement. She really had no other choice and finally moved her head. "Take off the tape, but one word and your son will disappear. You believe me?"

She nodded again, and he signaled his men. Zubict took the boy to the back of the house, and Rey enjoyed the panic in Brandie's eyes. Then the shock of pulling the tape made her wince in pain. To her credit, she closed her lips and swallowed any sound.

"I guess the next time I ask to come inside for a visit you'll allow it?" He shooed her backward with his hand until the back of her legs met the old chair in the corner. "I need my package. No more pretending you don't know what I'm talking about."

"But I don't. Really. If you would just tell me what to look for I—"

His palm slammed against her cheek to shut her up. The

sting didn't hurt as much as it empowered him. It dimly compared to the ecstatic surge he felt at being in control and slicing through her excuses.

"You can hit me all you want. If I don't know, I'll never have the answer you're looking for." She stuck her chin out, eyes closed, ready for another slap.

Rey unbuttoned his jacket and pulled his .45 from the shoulder holster. He stuck it under her chin. When the metal barrel connected with her skin, her eyes popped open with the knowledge that he could—and would—kill her.

"If you are of no use to me, then I could leave that boy in there an orphan." He leaned in closer so only she could hear him. "At least an orphan in everyone else's eyes. You and I know the truth. I will pull the trigger. Don't ever doubt that. I might reunite father and son."

He stood straight, twisting the barrel a little harder to make his point, then putting the pistol away.

"Was Glen working for you? If he left something at the café, it must still be there or someplace close. Tell me and I'll find it." Brandie's body showed her relief even if her words weren't grateful.

He believed her. He had her son, had control of her world. He looked around the four walls she called home. If their product had been sold, he would have heard about it. And there was nothing to indicate she'd come into cash. If she had, she would have ditched this town a long time ago and headed to a real city. She'd written about it in essays enough. Romanticizing history. It was the reason he'd given her a B in his class.

"Out." None of the men in his employment ever hesitated. He liked that. He heard the back door shut. "Cocaine. Thirty-five bricks of cocaine. It's been missing for seven months."

He could see the question in her eyes, but she didn't

voice it. Why was he looking for the shipment now? Why wait so long? Because it hadn't been his problem before last month. The organization made it his problem and promised more if he recovered it or the man who had stolen it.

"You don't need to know anything else. The less you know about this the better. If you do good, we might be able to use your place and give you a cut. I doubt your mechanic would have a problem with extra cash flow."

"I don't want your drug money. All I want is for you to get out of my life and leave us alone."

He slapped her again. Harder. This time silent tears fell across the bright pink staining her left cheek. She'd hold her tongue if she knew what was good for her.

Yes, he preferred for people to jump when he said jump. Give a directive and have it obeyed. He wouldn't tolerate anything else no matter who he ordered. His men were grateful to be employed and a part of his organization.

When he returned the cocaine to the men behind the curtain, he wouldn't need to hide behind boring history any longer. He would be making it. He'd say farewell to snotty college students.

"You seem to be forgetting that I'm the man who knows your secret, Brandie. The man who could destroy your world with one simple truth. I know the father of your child."

"So what? Why would anyone believe you? You don't have any proof."

"But I do." He sat on the broken-down couch. "Since you've been so reluctant to help me this past month, I decided to do a little research. You remember that research is my specialty, seeing that I'm a history prof and all."

"You're lying." She closed her eyes and stiffened, prepared for the slap he didn't deliver.

His cell notification let him know his men had successfully left the city limits. Time to let Brandie in on what they'd accomplished. "Test me and find out if I'm bluffing. It's a calculated move allowing you this much knowledge. I'm confident you'll come through for me."

"You are an arrogant bastard. I will never work for a drug dealer. You can never pay me enough."

He opened his cell to the picture sent by his men. Toby was lying on the floorboard. His distinctive blond hair sticking out beneath a greasy blanket.

"You're misunderstanding me, Brandie." He flipped the screen toward her. "Currently, the return of your son is the only payment I intend."

She leaped forward, and he recoiled quickly, but her short claws still managed to catch his neck. He pulled back his fist and hit her in the side of the head. She fell and was unconscious when he left her house.

Rey controlled himself and leisurely walked to the car, his fingers tapping the sting of scraped skin. Served the bitch right that he'd hit her. The feel of his gun reminded him how close he'd come to pulling it and ending her life. She had one chance to redeem her place in his game.

If she failed, his new weapon would get some practice.

Chapter Ten

It wasn't the first time Mitch had spent a day—or two—in jail. If he continued working undercover with the Rangers, it wouldn't be the last. He'd had a lot of interesting days for the past two and a half years as an undercover agent. His skills under the hood of a car made it easy to move up and down the Mexican border and Texas coastline.

If there was one thing Mitch had learned it was that there would always be more scum out there ready to step in and fill the gap of an organization that law enforcement brought down. He didn't know how Cord could work this job year after year. It seemed hopeless. Take out one bad guy, up pops another.

What was the point? People like Brandie and Toby were the point. He needed to get them someplace safe. Convince her that leaving was better for her and the kid. If only they knew what the former mechanic had hidden and where. He could return it, letting Cord know the details and maybe—just maybe—King would stop threatening Brandie.

"Bail's been posted, Striker," a deputy called from the hallway door to the holding cells. "Never had someone go to the trouble to post it anonymously before."

"About dang time," he muttered to himself, knowing that headquarters had come through.

The deputy took him through processing. The sheriff

impatiently waited on the other side of the cage, pacing, scrubbing his hand across his lower jaw. Something had happened. It couldn't be good if Pete was waiting to ask him for help.

Mitch stuffed his wallet into his back pocket and faced the barred door. The look of dread on his opponent's face made explanations unnecessary. Mitch's gut kicked acid into his throat. Toby. "They have the kid?"

Pete nodded, leading the way out of the jail. Just outside the door, he grabbed Mitch's arm. "If you have anything to do with Toby's kidnapping…"

"I don't." He looked the sheriff straight in the eyes. The urge to tell him he was one of the good guys was on the edge of his tongue. But he couldn't. Especially now. Keeping his cover was the only way to help Toby.

A craving to wring Rey King's neck overtook his thinking on the short ride to the house. He had no doubts that the wannabe mobster was behind the abduction.

"Can't help notice that you aren't curious about what happened, Striker." The sheriff put the car in Park and twisted in his seat, facing Mitch. "That might make me a bit suspicious."

"I was locked up in your jail. Might not have happened if I hadn't been."

"I figure you'd more than likely be dead before you let Toby be carried off." Pete scratched his chin with his thumb. "See, I have a feeling that Brandie's mixed up in something. We've had our fair share of excitement around here recently, but I'd have to be blind not to see that she's had more than the normal citizen."

"Meaning?" Mitch pressed his mouth shut tighter than before to keep his occupation a secret.

The house was surrounded with county vehicles. Deputies, the Quinns and neighbors were standing in the yard.

"She asked for you because she thinks you can help. You should convince her that I can help, too. I want to call in the Texas Rangers or the FBI."

He'd already decided to convince Brandie to use anyone who could help get her son back. His undercover position would be an asset, but they needed more eyes, more people searching for Toby. "What does she want?"

Pete shook his head. "I gather Brandie knows more about this situation than she's willing to tell. Brandie insisted you were the only person who could help her and magically bail is posted." Pete looked as angry as Mitch felt.

Brandie pushed open the screen door. Her body physically relaxed a little when their eyes met. He could see the reaction across the yard along with a swollen cheek where she'd been hit.

He wanted to shout who was to blame to every cop in the yard. To Brandie's father. To the town. They'd speed down the highway, find Rey King, get Toby back and the kidnapper would pay. He'd hurt. A lot.

They needed a case against him to put him away for good. Not just a trip to the hospital.

"I know you want explanations from me before we walk inside, but you won't get them." Brandie's eyes pleaded with him to remain silent. "It's not my story to tell."

"But you're admitting there *is* a story." Pete used a couple of four-letter words before he shoved open the Tahoe's door and stomped to the porch, waving off every question thrown his direction. "I need the family inside."

It was a hard call to make. Protect Brandie's right as a mother versus the need for the extra man power to find her son. Pete wasn't a dumb man. He knew something was going on and he'd figure it out sooner or later. He'd be more helpful and cooperative if Cord told him there was an undercover Ranger working in his town.

Revealing that was Cord's call. Mitch had already been reprimanded for telling Brandie. The family went into the living room.

"What are you doing to find my grandson?" Bud demanded from Pete, ignoring that Mitch slipped inside behind him to stand by Brandie.

"We've issued a statewide Amber Alert. To be honest, I wish you'd reconsider calling in the FBI. We don't have a lot of experience with kidnapping cases in Presidio County. We also have no idea what we're dealing with or why."

He and Brandie both knew who had her son. They both knew why. He needed to get her away from everyone so she could tell him the details.

"What do you mean reconsider the FBI? They haven't been called? What have you been doing for the past two hours? They could be across the blasted border with my grandson by now." Bud yelled at everyone, aiming his anger at Pete who was man enough to take it. Then he marched across the room finger pointing at his wife. "Did you know about this? How the hell are we supposed to find Toby if we don't know—"

The older man stopped himself, something clicking in his head. Mitch could see the gears turning and shoving information together. Bud looked over his shoulder and his eyes locked onto Mitch. The fright was masked with a desire to blame someone.

"Is this your fault?" the frantic man asked.

Brandie's hand swung out and caught Mitch's. He'd taken a step forward without realizing it. Pete came across the room to intercept him. He'd never felt the urge to defend himself from such an accusation before. People could normally call him every name in the book and he was able to ignore it. But Bud's question had insulted him like nothing he'd experienced.

Mitch drew a deep breath to calm down. Somebody needed to talk Bud into doing the same. But nobody else seemed willing.

So Mitch would. "I don't believe anyone here is responsible. We should let the sheriff explain what's being done and what they need from us."

The veins in Bud's neck might burst if they didn't get him calmed down. Six months working in the garage and he'd never lost his temper like this. And yet, no one in the room seemed very surprised.

Time for Mitch to keep his mouth shut and return to his role as the silent type staying on the edge of conversations, listening but not participating. He released Brandie's hand, crossed his arms and tried to look relaxed before he looked at the angel at his elbow.

Her eyes beseeched him. For help? For restraint? For…? She simply took his breath away and all thoughts along with it.

Brandie's mother cried softly into a handful of tissue. The conversation continued in the background between Pete and Bud. The only person who could change its direction was Brandie. She was exhausted and probably terrified. And unfortunately, she was as silent as him.

Mitch was getting lost in the blue of her eyes, trying to comfort her without a word when he heard his name pretty much taken in vain again.

"I still don't know what good you think this bum is going to do," Bud criticized, looking at Brandie. "You let him into your bed and he becomes the all-important person in your life."

"That's enough." Mitch's fingers balled into fists. He was conscious of the tense muscles in his arms. More aware that he was ready to take someone's head off as much as Bud. But he couldn't let anyone hurt Brandie more than she'd already been today. One look and a stranger would know she was a tear away from her breaking point.

"You ready to leave?" he asked her. Well, sort of asked her, since it came off more as *We're leaving whether you like it or not.* She nodded, then he turned to Pete. "Got a car to take us back to the garage? I don't think it's a good idea to walk."

"I'll do it myself."

"Good. We'll wait outside." He extended his hand and Brandie took it. Her parents watched, both silent until the door closed again and Bud continued his tirade. Harsh words. Mitch quickly got Brandie out of earshot.

"He doesn't mean anything. He's just upset and needs to do something." She tried to justify.

"I disagree with his methods. I'm also keeping my mouth shut. So should you until we know we're alone."

She waited on the Tahoe's backseat, looking older than she should with her thick hair pulled in a ponytail. The tiny studs in her ears were brightly colored rainbows. The earrings seemed at odds with their situation, but perfect for Brandie on a normal day.

She twisted the fake wedding ring on her slim finger instead of knotting the edge of her frilly shirt. It didn't make sense to wear a shirt like that to cook and serve customers at the café, but she liked them. She must since that's almost all she wore. That was it. It was the dang shirts that made her look older than twenty-four.

Personally, he enjoyed seeing her in funny T-shirts and faded torn jeans—even her cartoon pajamas. He also liked the glittery blue polish on her toenails that were currently covered by practical tennis shoes.

He'd never given much thought to what a woman wore.

A distraction from Toby's kidnapping? Maybe. Or a concentrated effort to keep from jumping in a car and heading for his kidnapper. If King's people hurt him, if he were traumatized in any way… Mitch wasn't normally a violent man. But the anger surged through him again. He felt his insides shake with the rage.

The emotional swell took him by surprise. Maybe Toby wasn't the only one with a crush. Cord had mentioned how the five-year-old was used to Mitch being a part of his life. Maybe it worked both ways. Maybe Mitch was used to the kid and Brandie being in his life, too.

"Nothing's going to happen to Toby. I promise you."

"You can't keep that promise, Mitch." The full pools in her eyes overflowed down her cheeks as she tilted her face toward his.

The bruising had begun. She needed ice to keep the swelling down. Someone had hit her. Didn't matter who, he'd make them pay at some point. He gently stroked her jawbone with his fingertip.

"Then I'll make one I can keep. I swear if he's hurt, the person responsible won't live to regret it."

Before she could object—which he assumed she would do by the O shape of her lips—the sheriff gestured for him to get in the truck.

PETE DROPPED THEM at the garage side door, but not before asking them again if they were ready to share their secret. Brandie kept her face turned away and stayed silent, fingers crossed that Mitch would do the same.

Pete told them that two deputies would stay at her house waiting for a call that wouldn't come from the kidnappers. The phone from the café had been forwarded there, as well. They were finished dusting for prints and searching inside.

Maybe this was so hard on Mitch because he had sworn

to uphold the law. A big part of her was grateful he had to keep secrets for a living. There was no one else she could turn to. If he was unwilling to help, she would be lost.

"Pete knows, doesn't he?" she said, but Mitch had stepped back into the garage. He hadn't heard her, but she already knew the answer. The sheriff might not know specifics, but he knew she was mixed up in something horrible.

He'd be watching as much as Rey's men.

With shaking hands, Brandie added coffee to the filter and cleared the broken glass from the pots. She found the extra carafe stashed deep on a shelf under the counter, rinsing, drying, then turning it on.

Black and blacker. That was the way Mitch liked his coffee. She didn't mind making him a cup while he inventoried his personal possessions.

Looking around the café depressed her. It wasn't just the overwhelming cleanup challenge that they faced. Its topsy-turvy shape represented her business and emotions... everything was so overwhelming.

Toby was gone. She'd put him in danger by being defiant to Rey. She dropped her face in her hands and cried. It was all her fault. If they didn't find Toby, no one else could be blamed. The decision was solely hers and it was too late to change her mind.

She had to pull herself back together. Fake composure. She heard Mitch's footsteps. "What doesn't kill ya makes you stronger. Right?"

Mitch's strong palm rubbed her back, patting it a couple of times like a guy completely uncomfortable with a crying female. But even in a pat, his strength was there, penetrating through the blouse she hated.

"What have I done? He's just five years old. He has to

be scared and wondering where I am. Oh, God. They might
have told him I was dead or don't want him. What if they
hurt him? What if you can't find him, Mitch?"

"I assume you have a message from King," he finally
said, completely ignoring all her doubtful thoughts. There
was no accusation in his voice or touch, just comfort. "Are
you sure you don't want to bring in outside help?"

"You are my help. Rey thinks you're just a mechanic.
He might believe you're still in jail. Won't that help us get
Toby back?"

He pulled a stool over for her to sit down.

"You know you don't have to rely just on me. One phone
call and the Texas Rangers will be searching for Toby. Are
you worried about your past coming out?"

"No. Nothing matters except Toby. Rey said he's watching, that he'll know if I do anything except bring him the
stupid package." Should she tell him that the package was
cocaine? Would he still help her?

"Did he tell you what's in this *package* or how big it
is?" Mitch took a clean bar towel, filled it with ice and
held it to her jaw.

"Wow, that really hurts."

"I'm guessing you haven't seen it yet?" Mitch's eyes
darted to the side of her face. "It should hurt awhile."

"No."

"You need to tell me the whole story."

Her body was stiff and sore from falling to the floor
when Rey had hit her. But the thought of telling Mitch
everything had her squirming on her stool. She'd shared
much more than she was comfortable with already.

"I told you—"

"Start with what's in the package. I can guess the rest."

He removed the ice and gingerly drew his knuckle along her cheek.

"Is it really bad?"

He grimaced and didn't need to answer. She took the ice pack and hoped it would help keep the swelling to a minimum.

"At least you don't need a straw. They could have broken your jaw. Want coffee or a milk shake? The freezer's messy, but they at least closed the door."

"Thank goodness. Coffee please. I made it strong so—"

"I know. You want it half with creamer." He shook the powdered mixture they used on the tables into a half-filled cup. He measured a spoonful of real sugar and then stirred.

Brandie realized it wasn't the first time he'd prepared her coffee. And it hit her that she hoped it wouldn't be the last. She wanted him to stick around—undercover Texas Ranger or true blue-collar mechanic. She liked Mitch. Period.

So why was she hesitating telling him the truth? Because she was afraid his secret profession would have to make the call to the authorities that they were looking for thirty-five bricks of cocaine. She didn't even know how much that meant.

If they found it—and they had no choice but to find it—he'd know what it was. She'd still be faced with convincing him to turn it over to Rey no questions asked.

"Stop debating with yourself and spill it. I've given you my word that I'd help. Before you think about how to ask…just ask me."

"What?"

"You want to know if I'm calling Cord if I find something illegal." He arched his eyebrows, asking the question with his face.

"Will you?"

"My first priority is to get Toby back. Second is to get the both of you to safety." He held up his hand. "Don't argue. Admit you're in danger. That's the deal. I find Toby and you both leave."

She hated to leave everything, but they'd have to. They just wouldn't be safe here anymore. She'd seen what happened to families that ticked off the Mexican cartel. Cord and Kate McCrea had lost their unborn child and nearly lost their lives. The illegal activity was higher now, putting more people at risk.

"You're right," she reluctantly admitted, dropping the cold pack to the counter. But what Mitch didn't know was that she and Toby had nowhere to run.

"After I see to both of those, then I'll settle the score with King." Mitch barely touched her chin, taking another look at her bruise. "You hungry? How 'bout a grilled cheese and then we get started looking for that package."

"Sounds like a plan. I'll get the stovetop cleaned up if you get the cheese from the walk-in."

Mitch led the way as she fought more tears. It had been a long time since anyone was so completely on her side. She swiped at the wetness trickling down her face before turning on the flattop. Nothing happened. "Great. I need to flip the breaker."

"I can get it. Stay there."

She cleared a work area, wiped off the cast iron and found the bread.

"Brandie!" Mitch called.

She ran to the back of the garage where the breaker box was located. Mitch stood in front of the shelf, staring at the wall, rubbing the back of his neck. Brandie picked her way through the old boxes of car parts that had been brushed off the shelves.

"All the breakers are marked. So what's the problem?"

"Do you know what this box is for?" He pointed to one that had been hidden behind the car parts. "It's disconnected."

"It must be to the old pit bay. Dad sealed that up years ago when he bought the lift that you use now." She'd been eleven or twelve. Her mom ran the café and her dad ran the garage. They couldn't afford sitters—she'd insisted she was too old for them anyway. So she'd sat in the corner booth finishing homework, listening to the jukebox and overhearing all the town gossip.

"Makes sense to disconnect it. But this is newer wiring than the rest. It looks like it's been used recently. Maybe just before I arrived?"

"You mean Glen tried to repair something. That would be unusual for him. He hardly did anything without Dad's instructions."

"Maybe he didn't want your dad to know."

"You mean, you think he's hiding something down there. But why wouldn't he come back to get it?" She sank to a stack of tires as the realization hit her. Glen couldn't come back. "He's dead. Rey killed him. That's how he knows his drugs are still here at the garage. You knew. That's why you came to work here and have been tricking me."

Mitch searched through strewn tools. She stared at him as he found and connected a power drill, then began unscrewing the metal plating that covered the pit bay.

"Yes, he was murdered. Yes, his death presented an opportunity for me to observe. I didn't want to trick you. I hope you believe me."

Brandie was stunned. "There's too much to take in. Toby has been kidnapped and is being held for the ransom of thirty-five cocaine bricks that my murdered former mechanic hid in my father's garage. Oh, and let's not forget that the mechanic I could have very much become involved with—and who I've admired tremendously—has been lying to me for six months. Because he's one of the good guys, an actual-to-goodness Texas Ranger playing undercover and sleeping on my couch."

Chapter Eleven

Mitch stopped retracting screws from the steel plating.

"Thirty-five? King told you there's thirty-five bricks of cocaine down here?" He wanted to react to her slip about the possibility that they could become involved. It wasn't the time. He had to let it go and only think about Toby.

"Rey didn't know where it was, just that I have to find it if I want Toby back. We don't know that it's down here."

"That's around a million dollars street value. That's more than enough evidence to put him away for a very long time."

He continued removing the screws, pretty certain Brandie hadn't realized she'd even spoken her complaint out loud. He would deal with it later. He had to finish one job before starting another. Toby, drug smugglers, then a possible relationship with Brandie. He was looking forward to that.

"It's not evidence. It's ransom. We have to turn it over to them."

"I need to call Cord to document—"

"No!" She jumped to her feet, hands karate-chopping the air. "We play this completely by Rey King's rules and we get my son back."

He stood with every intention of going to her, calming her down, assuring her that he'd never do anything to put Toby in jeopardy. Instead, he just stood there. Holding on to the cord, he let the electric impact wrench slide and clang on the floor.

"If you can't do this my way, then you need to leave. Right now. Just go." She bent to pick up the wrench.

"That isn't an option." He pulled on the cord, drawing her close enough to wrap in his arms and rest his chin on the top of her head.

The tears that had threatened fell again.

She clung to the electric wrench and buried her face in his shirt. Completely lost, he just held Brandie tight. Unlike the last time he'd been around a woman crying. Not since junior high when his dad had moved out. His mother had cried for days even though it had been her yelling for his dad to get out. All Mitch had done was cover his head with a pillow.

That wasn't an option at the moment.

"I'll get Toby back," he said softly across her head after the tears had lessened. "I have to do my job, too."

Her body and cheek were flush with him when she said, "What happens when this is all over and Rey finds out you're a Ranger? What do you think he'll do then?"

"No one will know."

"I can't risk it. He'll kill us. All of us. That's what monsters like him do when they get angry. We see it all the time."

"That's on the other side of the border." He bent his knees to look her in the eyes. "The Rangers can relocate you, put you in protection. Would it be such a bad thing?"

At the moment, Mitch couldn't imagine walking back into the same room as Bud Quinn. After the things he'd said about Brandie, how would she ever forgive him?

She shoved him away and gripped the wrench tighter, dragging the cord across the concrete floor. "This is my home. Do you really think I could just walk away from everything I've ever known? Or take Toby away from his grandparents?"

"But you just said a minute ago—"

It didn't make sense and wouldn't. No one should go through the stress she was under at the moment. One of the strongest people he'd ever met turned from him and stared out the rear window. No one was out there. Just a small gravel lot where their cars were parked.

She needed a minute to come back around. He was glad they were here instead of at her house with the Quinns. Her dad reminded him of his own father.

His parents hadn't had a pleasant divorce. Years of screaming were followed by years of complaints about each other. It made undercover work all that more appealing. Like Brandie, he hadn't had any siblings. No one else shared the burden of their constant bickering. It fell on his shoulders and he learned real quick to not give either parent ammo about the other.

But Brandie's parents were essentially blackmailing her as much as King was. If she stepped out of line, she'd lose everything. Why didn't she see it that way?

"You should leave. Before you find out if anything's under those pieces of thick steel. Go." She stared out the window. Not facing him.

"Is that what you really want?"

He wasn't leaving. There was no way he could leave her to face King by herself. But something in him pushed her for an answer. He wanted to hear her decision and wanted her to need him to stay. That particular emotion had never crept to the surface before.

Need? Want? Desire? These weren't normal emotions for an undercover Ranger.

Damn.

"You shouldn't go against your principles, Mitch. If you have to tell Cord about the missing drugs, then so be it." She was killing him with kindness. "But I'm afraid you'll have to come back with a warrant."

She was working him like a problem customer. That's what she did, and he admired her ability to be gracious and disagree at the same time.

"It hasn't escaped me that you are still holding that impact wrench. I imagine it's to keep me from using it. So I'll ask again. Do you want me to leave?"

Her hands shook as her knuckles turned white. She clenched her jaw and visibly swallowed. All signs of someone trying hard not to say what they really want.

"Brandie, honey." He crossed the short distance to her again. "I'm here for you and Toby. I might get fired for my divided loyalties, but I heard of this great mechanic's job, room and board included. Sounds like heaven."

The little spitfire hugged the wrench to her chest, shaking her head, sort of laughing and crying at the same time. "I can't ask—"

"Doesn't seem like you did." He squeezed her shoulders with his hands, squelching the desire to pull her to his chest yet again. "I volunteered. Now if you'll give back the wrench, I can see if we can stop looking for King's cocaine."

He extended his hand, and the power wrench was popped into his palm. That same look of relief she'd displayed on her porch at the sight of him this morning relaxed her features and her body. It was crazy, but he felt the same way. If she'd kicked him out, he might have thrown away his badge to stay.

Insane was a better word that came to mind to describe his decision. Or maybe stupid. Like he'd said to her inside the café, one phone call and the resources of the state of Texas would be at their service.

He knelt by the steel plates to remove the last few screws. "I must be crazier than I look."

"Well, I don't know, Mitch. You're acting about as crazy as me." She began clearing the floor, picking up parts, setting them on the shelves.

"Last one. Brandie?"

Her hands encircled her neck, and she looked toward the ceiling. "Change your mind?" She dropped her hands, slapping her thighs before she looked at him.

"Nope. I'm not calling for backup. I'm not going to stop the exchange and we're going to get Toby back. I'll be with you a hundred percent of the time. No exceptions."

"Great. Can we see if it's even there?"

He knew it was the only place it could be. "I'm going to document the money. Rey King is going to jail and this will put him there."

Her eyes closed as she took in a deep breath. "So be it. I just want my son back safely in my arms."

He took his phone from his pocket, took pictures and then removed the last screw. The plating had been screwed to a wooden frame first covered in plywood to make it safe to walk in the shop. The length and weight of the frame should have been impossible to lift. But under the metal cover, the plywood had been cut. Two finger holes made it possible to lift, revealing the ladder underneath.

"This is it." Mitch took a couple of pictures and lifted the wood, then took a few more of the pit. "Empty."

Brandie was just behind his shoulder. "Glen wouldn't have gone to all this trouble to hide nothing."

"There's no guarantee that whoever killed him doesn't have the cocaine."

"It's kind of dark down there. I'll grab a flashlight." She ran into the café.

There wasn't a question of whether he was going or not. He just didn't want Brandie to fall apart when they didn't find anything. He was already on the top rungs when she handed him a tiny penlight from her key ring.

"Take pictures, will ya?" He held out his phone.

She slid his cell into her pocket and sat on the side, ready to come over the edge. "Don't even argue with me. You might miss something."

She shimmied down the ladder faster than he could figure out how to turn the flashlight on by twisting the end cap. It was close quarters, barely enough room for a man his size to maneuver comfortably. And man alive was he uncomfortable with Brandie down there with him.

"Looks like you should have connected that wire. Then maybe these fluorescents would come on." She flipped a switch up and down but nothing happened.

It was dark, so looking at all the notches on the wall would take a few minutes. Brandie stuck out her hand, and he gave her the light. She immediately walked to the far end.

"Oh, my gosh, Mitch. That's a handle. Can you reach it?"

"Stand back. If it's a block of cement then I'm going to control where it lands. Doesn't make sense, though. It would be too heavy for one man to move."

He yanked, and a square board smeared with concrete pulled away. Along with a stack of cash and a couple of .38 Specials, there was a duffel filling the entire back of the hole. The light flashed on his cell. Brandie was taking the pictures, documenting what they found.

He reached for the bag but hesitated. The urge to call Cord grew. Along with a very bad feeling. Nothing tangible. He just knew something was going to go wrong if they didn't bring the Rangers on board.

"Aren't you going to see what's inside?" She stretched her hand toward the bag.

"Wait. Did King tell you when to meet?"

"Yes. I'm supposed to call and meet later today if I find the package."

"Then we're going to need proof."

"Of what?" she asked as he tugged her back toward the ladder. "No. You're trying to convince me to call the law. To let your friends handle this. Rey said I'd never see Toby again. Do you want that on your head?"

"You came to the conclusion that Pete knew what was going on. He didn't hang around and he didn't leave a deputy to stay with you. Your son's been kidnapped and he didn't leave anyone here to see if you would be contacted. That's not procedure in any law enforcement agency." Mitch's jaw muscle twitched as he ground his molars together.

"That…that doesn't mean anything."

Mitch took her hand in his. Her hands were chilled from the coolness in the pit or maybe holding the ice earlier. "He knows something's up and he's trying to trap us for some reason." He released her hand and rubbed the back of his neck.

As dark as it was, he could see the slight shake of her head as she acknowledged his idea, but still tried to ignore it. At the bottom of the ladder, he waited for her to grab the rung. She shrugged off his hand.

"You're wrong. He wouldn't do that. We've known each other forever."

"Brandie, he's a cop. He's doing his job and he wouldn't be worth his salt if he couldn't figure out someone's threatening you."

Her hand covered her cute little O-shaped mouth. She got it and he hated springing it on her. Right then in a car repair pit, with the smell of a decade of grease, oil and other smells...all he wanted to do was comfort her. Make her believe everything would be all right. Convince her beyond a shadow of a doubt that he had the answers.

He did. But she wasn't going to like them.

"What do we do?" she asked softly.

"First, I'm putting everything back the way it was. Wait for it." He pressed a finger to her lips at the first inhaled breath or objection. "Then we make a video of coming down here and finding everything. We document our movements. You admit that you're being forced to cooperate in order to get your son back."

"You're treating me like a criminal."

"We can't prove these drugs aren't yours. We have to do this my way to protect you." And put Rey King in jail.

"Why don't *you* believe they belong to me?"

"The thought never crossed my mind." Mitch handed her the penlight. "Hold that, will ya?"

She stayed put while he put the wall cover back in place. She didn't wait for instructions after he was done. Flashlight off, she climbed out of the pit. He followed and put everything back in place while she searched for something on his phone. She wouldn't find anything except a few random pictures of Toby or a car.

It seemed a little ridiculous, but he put every screw back in place. He wanted her name squeaky clean. The way he felt about her, having already been reprimanded for blowing his cover—to her... Yeah, he had to think about protecting her from future accusations.

"We need his fingerprints," she said out of the blue. "Do you know how to lift prints? It's okay, I've looked it up on the internet. We've got everything we need here."

"That's a smart idea." He stuck out his hand for the cell, switching it to video. "If something goes wrong. Hey, I'm not saying it will. But if something goes wrong, this may help find Toby. You ready?"

The video captured all the raw emotion Brandie was experiencing and the purple-colored jaw from where she'd been hit. She explained everything pertinent to the case. She didn't need to mention that King had threatened to expose her son's parentage. This would be enough.

When they were done, he sent the file to a secure email account. "You're positive you don't want to involve anyone else for help or even backup?"

"We can't." A simple statement of fact this time.

"Then let's get started."

Mitch opened everything again while Brandie held the phone, recording. They found a regular-sized flashlight, which brightened everything once they were down the ladder. And this time, he took the money and gun out of the homemade wall safe and wrapped them in his shirt until they could secure a substitute evidence bag.

Back upstairs, Brandie found his charger still plugged into the wall so they could continue recording. He set the duffel on the bed. She stayed his fingers on the zipper.

"What if this isn't the drugs?"

"Only one way to find out."

There was no reason to second-guess themselves. The bag was stuffed to capacity. If King was missing thirty-five bricks of cocaine, this was probably it.

"Let's make that fingerprint powder and get this over with." She turned off the camera on the cell and dropped it to the mattress.

As she sorted through the rubble in the café for what she needed, Mitch swiped the video record button, switching the image to record himself.

"Cord, this was the best I could do. If the exchange for Toby goes wrong or if something happens to me… For the record and without a gun to my head, this video should serve as my last will and testament. I want Brandie Ryland to receive my benefits and savings. I'm counting on you, man, as one Ranger to another, that you'll get Brandie and her son out of this mess here in Marfa. Make sure she's safe for me."

Chapter Twelve

"Patrice, my love. I missed you last night." Rey waltzed into the kitchen as if he didn't have a care in the world. At least not the version he lived in. Patrice had already learned about how he'd messed things up.

The Amber Alert on her phone had awoken her hours ago from a sound sleep, notifying the entire state of Texas of Toby Ryland's disappearance.

Patrice's world had been missing thirty-five bricks of cocaine for far too long. The filthy mechanic had managed to hide it from them, and Rey had been too quick with his death. The drugs had to be at the café. It was the last possible place they could be hidden. Rey had complicated everything with this kidnapping.

The buyers had expected the cocaine in their hands weeks ago and were becoming impatient. She could placate them for only so long and it looked like time had run out. But kidnapping the boy had never been part of their strategy to find it.

Rey kissed her on the cheek, greeting her much like a longtime boyfriend should. They'd been together for three very long, tedious years. She took a sip of her coffee, and as was his custom, he swung around to her back, dropping his hands to caress her bare breasts beneath her robe.

"Slow down." She shrugged away and pulled the robe closed. "What happened last night?"

He leaned on the kitchen bar next to her and snagged the last piece of her bacon from her plate. She absolutely hated when he ate her food. She hated a lot of things about Rey King. Too many to think upon at the moment.

It had been months since she'd been satisfied—sexually or in her everyday routine. She loved variety in her life and bed. It was definitely time for a change. Time to make her move and prove who'd been running the show all along.

"We snatched the kid. So I figure we'll have the blow by this afternoon."

He'd purposefully deviated from her plan. She was furious and couldn't show it. The time wasn't right. He might get the wrong idea and realize that the Chessmen organization was as fictitious as his brains.

"Rey, baby." She laid on the thick accent he liked that was a very sad Marilyn Monroe. "Do you think the men in charge are going to get mad, sug? I mean, they said to bust some stuff up, but what if the kid's mom lets the police help find him? Things could get real complicated. Will there be extra cops and state troopers on the highways?"

"Their way was too slow. We got the kid. I guarantee we'll have the cocaine by tonight."

He kissed her and slid his hands under the silky material again. The Marilyn imitation always got him turned on. And if he was thinking with one certain piece of his anatomy, he wouldn't be thinking with any other. Some men were so easily manipulated. And even more loved the dumb blonde she could imitate so well.

"There's nothing to worry your pretty head about. The guys and I got this covered. They have true incentive to find that million in cocaine now. It'll be in their hands before we're finished in the other room." He tugged her up and with him toward his bed.

Patrice followed. Sex allowed her time to think. They passed through the door, he stripped off her robe and threw her to the mattress.

"Are you high, Rey?"

He ripped the buttons, pulling his shirt apart. "Yeah, baby, want some? I got more in my pocket than what you're craving."

Craving? He couldn't give her what she craved, but he'd do. "I'm fine like this." She grabbed his belt before he could toss it away.

"Oh, yeah, baby. You're always fine." He buried his face between her breasts and rolled on top of her.

While she let him have his way, she'd put together a new strategy. Then she'd have her real fun.

Chapter Thirteen

Brandie paced, turned circles, tapped her toes and then a pen, waiting on Mitch to finish fingerprinting the bags. She'd obviously been distracting since he'd set his phone in a place to record him without being held. She didn't mean to be in such a hurry but not doing anything to get her son back was more nerve-racking than handling the drugs themselves.

"I think I should call Rey and tell him we've found the bag." Brandie watched him carefully brush away the fingerprint powder that they'd made. "We can at least set up a time for the exchange."

"Not until I'm finished with this." He waved his fingers over the cocaine. He wore two layers of food service gloves, trying not to mar any prints left behind. And not leave his prints to confuse police officers later.

"Wasn't twenty-five of those brick things plenty? You've said they must have been wearing gloves. You haven't found anything but a smudge so far." She picked up the second paintbrush they'd found with Toby's art supplies. "I could do a couple."

"It's better if I do them all."

"So you said. They won't question anything if you're the only one who attempts to lift the prints. But you're taking hours. I want my son back. Today."

Mitch didn't say anything. He stopped the recording, saved it to the cloud and began everything again.

"Do you have enough candle soot?" She'd blackened a plate more times than she could count with their emergency candles. If he needed more, she'd have to go to the gift shop on the corner.

"I think so."

"I'm going to clean up the front then."

"Good idea."

She'd tried several times to clean up the café dining room without success. Usually a very patient person, today she wanted to get her son. Nothing else mattered. Looking at the mess in front of her dampened her spirits again. It was so overwhelming.

One thing. Concentrate on one thing and finish it.

She gathered all the condiments that belonged on the tables. Two were missing so she began in a corner and searched methodically. She felt like Mitch as he had checked each inch of the plastic wrapping on each brick of drugs. She found them under the fourth booth.

The blouse that her mom had given her caught on something and ripped. She kept a spare set of clothes in the back and changed. Getting into comfortable jeans and a T-shirt shifted her attitude. Then her stomach growled.

The thought of her little boy going hungry curled her fingers into fists. She didn't want to think about being comfortable or about food. But if they were going to meet drug dealers it should probably be on a full stomach.

At least the kitchen wasn't torn to pieces. She tied a cook apron around her waist and wiped the remaining flour off the flattop. While it heated, she picked up pans from the floor and stacked them near the sink, then gathered her ingredients. Just as she put the sliced turkey and buttered bread on the hot surface, she heard a knock on the front window.

Her heart raced, and she couldn't breathe. Her first instinct was to run to the garage and to Mitch. Rey had to be back. Then logic kicked in. He wouldn't knock and wouldn't be seen coming through the front door. She kept the metal spatula in her hand and slowly peeked through the service window.

Pete stood at the door, knuckle rapping against the glass again. "Mitch!" she called loudly. "The sheriff's here."

She had to let him inside. She didn't have any choice. Did she? No. She flipped the dead bolt and prayed Mitch had enough time to put the drugs away. "We're not open."

"I know you're not open, Brandie. We thought you needed to know what could be happening." He turned sideways, and she could see Cord standing a few feet behind him. A café regular walked down the sidewalk, peering into her window to get a peek at the wreckage.

"I appreciate you coming by but today's not— I'm just really not up to...um...company."

"Any news, Sheriff?" Mitch asked from over her head.

"We need to come inside." Pete said the words, but Cord arched an eyebrow and nodded his head slightly.

Mitch must have received the message from his boss and pushed open the door. Brandie shot him a look, silently asking if he were crazy but he missed it. He shook the hands of the two men and flipped undamaged chairs around for everyone to sit down.

This was not how her afternoon was supposed to go. What if Rey had men watching the café?

"Mitch, will you help me with the sandwiches?"

"Sure."

"You guys help yourself to some coffee. You might have to rinse out a cup but the pot's fresh." She took her mechanic's hand and kept him next to her so he couldn't even hint at or tell either man about the cocaine.

"The bread is practically burned." She flipped the sandwiches and turned off the flattop.

"It's okay. I just need to shove something into my stomach. It doesn't matter if it tastes good. I'll find some plates."

"Just grab the box of to-go wrappers." She accepted the thin aluminum sheets he handed her and scooped the sandwich onto it. She lowered her voice. "What do you think they want?"

Mitch shrugged with a mouthful of turkey and cheese. "Why don't we ask 'em?"

He ambled comfortably into the other room, seeming completely at ease facing two law enforcement officers with a million dollars' worth of cocaine in the next room. There was no way she could look as calm and collected as he did. She was more nervous than words to describe it. But she should be. Her son had been kidnapped.

Mitch was right. All they could do was ask her and all she had to do was not answer. So she followed him. He inhaled his sandwich—burned bread and all—while she nibbled, too sick at her stomach to think anything would actually stay down.

Mitch stopped and got them both glasses of water. Brandie stayed at the counter watching three lawmen sizing each other up. Who would break the silence first?

"Why are you here?" she finally asked. The little bit of sandwich in her tummy turned to a rock waiting on the answer.

"To try and talk some sense into you." Pete flattened his palm on the table.

Cord pressed his lips together into a thin line and flicked some imaginary crumbs on the table. Mitch twirled the bottom of his glass in a circle after he sat down and used that patience thing where he never seemed in a hurry to get anything done. Which was so opposite to all that he accomplished every day.

"So talk." Mitch leaned back, and the front feet of his chair left the floor. He looked totally relaxed with his arms crossed, his pointer finger tapping on his biceps.

Pete leaned on the tabletop, his head quirked to the side looking at her mechanic. Not knowing that Mitch was much more than his outward appearance or his calm collective.

"Don't convince *me*," he said, nodding his head in her direction. "She's calling the shots."

Yep, Mitch was a man of his word and definitely her friend.

Silence. The bite she was chewing turned into a piece of dried-up jerky. And they all waited. Mitch's finger didn't miss a beat to whatever rhythm he was tapping on his arm. She finally swallowed but still didn't know what to say.

"I thought you came here to talk." She gulped some water to get the awful flavor of burned toast from her taste buds.

"I brought Cord out here to convince you that you need help with whatever you're supposed to do with the people who took Toby. You've got to realize it's too dangerous to work on your own."

"Why do you assume I'm supposed to do anything?"

Pete pushed away from the table, slapping it at the same time he stood. "I'm not a fool and I'm not your father who's too upset to see straight. I'm the sheriff. And he's a Texas Ranger."

It took her a second to realize he meant Cord, not Mitch.

"You can't do anything—"

"And yet you've chosen the help of a drifter mechanic with anonymous friends who post his bail."

"There's nothing—"

"If he's a part of whoever's threatening you, or working with whoever has taken Toby, I swear, bail or no bail, I'll get him behind bars. Nobody should mess with a kid." He yanked Mitch to his feet with two fistfuls of fabric.

"Pete, please stop." She was speaking to the sheriff but pleaded silently with the Ranger who still sat there with an unconcerned expression. "Cord? Do something."

He fiddled with the hat that Rangers were so famous for, changing its angle on the table, then scratching his chin as if he weren't concerned. Mitch's hands slowly wrapped around Pete's wrists, tilting them backward. They were about to have it out.

"Just stop!" she yelled to prevent the all-out fight that was bound to happen.

"What's he forcing you to do, Brandie?"

"Oh, for goodness' sakes. This is so ridiculous. I should be taking care of my son, not supervising grown men acting his age."

"Tell me what he's making you do and I'll help you get Toby back," Pete said with a grimace of pain.

"You can't. Mitch knows what he's doing. Please let him go."

Cord jumped up, his chair falling backward to the floor. "You win, Pete. Mitch works for me. He's an undercover member of our task force. I'm not sure how this relates to Toby's kidnapping, but Brandie found out last night. That's probably why she wants his help."

"I knew it!" the sheriff boasted.

Pete and Mitch dropped their hands, both taking a step in retreat, both mumbling under their breath.

"Dammit. I said you were getting too involved." Cord turned to Mitch. "What the hell's going on and why does Brandie need your help?"

Mitch shrugged. "Not my story to tell."

"Will someone tell me why we've blown the cover on a major operation?" Cord commanded with authority. "Is someone going to explain why? And it better be worth it."

"Oh, my gosh. You all just need to stop. Please just stop." She stomped as loud as she could to the door and put her hand on the knob. "I get that this reveal allows you to be the best of pals. We can schedule a playdate for later. Get out. Now. Before someone sees you here."

"Who?" Pete and Cord asked together.

Mitch pulled her away from the door to whisper in her ear, "We're good. It's still your decision. You're in charge and I'll do what you want even if they order me not to."

They looked at each other, and she shook her head. She couldn't risk never seeing Toby again.

"I know someone's forcing you to do something illegal." Pete was quiet and firm and sounded sad. "Let me help you."

"I'm waiting on the kidnappers to contact me. You know why I couldn't do it at the house. Dad would have just kept getting worse."

Pete and Cord nodded their heads.

"I'm not saying that I've been contacted. But if I am, I'll do exactly what they say to do. I want my son back and I'll do anything to hold him again. Period. End of story."

Mitch laced his fingers through hers and the steadying strength she'd felt so many times in the past day filled her being. She could calmly take a moment and believe everything would be okay.

"They don't know I'm undercover. Our operation hasn't been blown. Yet." His fingers tightened around hers. "If they're watching this place, it's going to be hard to explain why you've been here so long. So maybe it's time for you both to leave?"

"You going to leave this alone, Pete?" Cord asked, settling his hat on his head, ready to leave.

"I don't have too much of a choice. We haven't had any hits from the Amber Alert."

"You think I'm making a mistake. I have to trust myself, Pete. How many times have these men attacked our town? How many times will they hurt someone in our future? I know you want to put them away forever, but I can't risk Toby's life with that possibility."

Chapter Fourteen

"You can make your call now, but use my phone." Mitch told Brandie as he zipped the duffel, mentally retracing his entire process. He'd been painstakingly slow and careful. Driving Brandie nuts while she waited, but still methodical. He hadn't messed it up.

Granted, he wasn't a fingerprint expert, but he'd found no useable prints or even smudges. He'd finished up after Cord and Pete left, cursing under his breath that there was nothing to tie King to the drugs or Glen's death. But more so that his cover had been blown.

He was a professional who had been undercover for more than two years. He'd never blown it before. Then again, a five-year-old's life had never been at stake. Or someone like Brandie.

How many people did he know who could come through this ordeal without falling apart? Very few individuals had the rare inner strength that he admired in her. There wasn't anything about her he didn't appreciate.

Maybe her stubbornness to trust him, but even that was explained by her past. He'd find out that entire story someday. A barrier would be crossed when she shared that part of herself. And for the first time in his life he was willing to see what was on the other side.

"We've got a lot of hours ahead of us to get both places

back up and running." Brandie stretched on his cot, waking from a short nap while she'd waited.

He looked around the garage, seeing the needless destruction but it didn't compare to the café. Amazed that she still thought she could come back here and take up her life as if nothing happened.

"Where's your phone?" she asked, pulling hers from her jeans pocket.

He handed her the cell from the shelf and waited for her to tap in the number. Then he covered her hand, delaying the conversation with King.

"Look, Brandie, my cover's done here. I'm taking this money and getting Toby back." He was starting to like that cute little O shape she made when she was taken by surprise. "Don't try to argue. You'll tell King you're being followed. This is the deal. He wants the cocaine, he gets me."

"Whoa, now—"

"That's the only way." He squeezed her hand, fighting the urge to take her in his arms.

She stood and took a couple of steps away from him. "I appreciate that you want to keep me safe, but you're mistaken if you think you have the right to order me to do anything. I thought I made it perfectly clear that we'd do everything the way Rey tells us to. I'm following his instructions to the letter and that's it."

"I wasn't trying to order you."

"It's okay." She patted his chest as she passed by and crooked a finger for him to follow to the garage office. "We follow his instructions."

A petite fireball. That's exactly who Brandie Ryland was. First the phone call, then he'd tie her up and leave her on the cot in order to prevent her from being in danger.

Too involved. Yep, Cord had called it right. Brandie and

Toby were more important to him than the case. He knew it and it didn't matter.

She dialed the cell. Someone answered and immediately hung up. "That's the number he gave me to call. Should I use my phone?"

"Give him a second, then call again and tell him your name. He should realize that you can't use your own phone because of the cops."

She did. Someone answered and she put the call on speaker.

"Brandie, Brandie, Brandie. My men tell me you had visitors and haven't left your pathetic café all day. Are you calling to tell me you can't give me what I want?"

"I found your bag of drugs. Tell me how to get my son back." Brandie shook the phone like it might be King's head.

"We tore that place apart. Glen must have had a real good hiding place."

Mitch silently moaned, realizing he should have recorded the conversation. It would have cleared Brandie of any wrongdoing and would have given the Rangers enough for a warrant. He was definitely off his game.

Sharing that he was undercover with—at the time—their prime suspect. Then staying and protecting Brandie and leaving this place wide-open… He had to set the emotional attachments aside and perform like a true professional.

"Enough with the nice stuff!" she yelled. "I want my son."

"Simmer down. You and your mechanic take his car. Drive around so you know no one's following you. Be at the south end of Nopal Road at five o'clock. Then start walking east." King disconnected.

"Do you know where Nopal Road is?" He pocketed his

phone, knowing that he had to notify Cord about the drop and send him access to his secure account.

She nodded. "We won't have cell service since it's out in the middle of nowhere."

"What *is* out there?" He put the location into his cell.

"Nothing. I don't think there's even a tree large enough to hide behind."

"That's not in our favor. It's also not good that they want the both of us in my car. He's smart enough not to want any surprises, like me surprising them after we have Toby."

"If we're supposed to drive around for a couple of hours, maybe you should fill the gas tank."

"Just in case they strand us out there for a while, would you get together some water and food? I'll move the car inside the garage." He lifted shelving and took a push broom to make a clear path for both cars.

Before turning the key he looked under the carriage and hood of his car. He removed a false bottom and took out his satellite phone and a tracking device. He wouldn't notify Cord until the last minute, but he had sworn an oath to uphold the law. Letting King abscond with a million in cocaine wouldn't work for the state of Texas.

The part of him that still had brains wanted to know why King had specifically said to use his car. As far as his eyes could tell, there weren't any explosives or a tracker. He cranked the engine, moved to the pumps, filled up and moved inside the empty bay.

He repeated everything with Brandie's car, reversing it over the steel plates he hadn't secured back in place. Brandie had a box of fruit and sandwiches. On top of the sleeping bag she'd taken from his cot, she set Toby's backpack with his toys and crayons inside.

"I need my cell." She extended her palm. Determined. Not waiting for him to ask what for.

He had an idea that she was calling home. Her dad could yell and be full of bluster. He could lay down extensive rules and limitations. But bottom line, he was still her dad. Her parents loved her and Toby.

He put their emergency supplies in the backseat, paying close attention to the phone call behind him.

"Hi, Dad. Yeah, sorry about this morning. Everything's crazy. I know you love him. And me."

There was a long pause when Brandie listened and was more patient than Mitch could ever have been.

"I called to check in and let you know that…that Pete is keeping me up-to-date here at the café. I love you, too." She turned to Mitch, her eyes once again brimming with tears. "I couldn't risk telling him. I wanted to, but couldn't. I hope they'll both forgive me."

"You're going to bring Toby back and be a hero. No one will question what you had to do to achieve that."

"I hope you're right because at this exact moment, looking at that bag and the secrets it has… I feel like a lowlife drug dealer." She crossed her arms, pushing her breasts up under the T-shirt.

"You remember what you told me earlier today. You'll do anything to get your son back. Most good parents would, too."

"If we head north, getting back to Nopal Road will take a couple of hours. Should we grab a map?" She gestured to the garage office where they were sold.

"I have a detailed map of the area under the seat. You ready?"

"Yes. Everything's already locked up. We just have to set the alarm."

"Then let's go get Toby."

Chapter Fifteen

Rey looked so pleased with himself. It had been easy for Patrice to get his consent to come along. Normally, she let someone else take care of the mundane deals. But today was exciting.

Today, all her patience and bowing to inferior partners would pay off.

Today, Patrice Orlando would become queen of her world by taking control of the board and all the chessmen. That was a logical assumption.

Nothing would stop her. Especially not Rey King and his insignificant kidnapping exchange. He thought recovering the cocaine would set him in the sights of the bigger distributors. No, the cocaine was a distraction to keep him sidetracked.

All it did was square them for the next and biggest delivery they'd attempted. But she hated to be rushed. Hastily laid plans were how she normally took out an opponent. Rey had set her plan in motion earlier than she'd wanted, but she'd deal with it. She always dealt with it.

She smoothed her stocking as she formulated a plan around at least two questions. First, whether to keep the couple alive or not. And secondly, to return the boy or keep him for leverage. If she kept him, she'd need to use that leverage within twenty-four hours. Waiting any longer would just bring the law breaking down her door or whatever door she hid the kid behind. No matter what branch of the police it was, she couldn't afford to have her operation slowed.

Yes, today was her new beginning, and she wouldn't let Rey screw it up with this unplanned kidnapping exchange. He'd end up bragging to someone about how easy the entire debacle was to pull off. They in turn would bring the police into the picture. Now that they'd arrived at the drop, step one would be to goad him into handling things himself.

Sitting as close as they were, it was easy to turn her body into his, to sensually cradle his bare arm between her breasts and scoot his hand into her lap.

"Rey, this is so exciting. In all the years that we've been together, I've never really seen you so in charge." She grazed her nails across the knit shirt he wore, drawing a pattern to his slacks and then back up. "It's so…sexy."

"You want to see me more in charge than just talking about it?"

"Baby, you've got men to pick up the money for you. What if something goes wrong?" she deliberately pursed her lips. She wanted the fake tears so none of Rey's crew would suspect anything. So she thought back to when she had nothing. A run-down shack of a house. A father who loved to smack her around. She rubbed her cheek, remembering the sting.

"Brandie's easily manipulated, barely a challenge to me. She just wants her kid back. The guys have been watching her all day. They haven't made a call or contacted the police."

"Are you sure?" She smiled as big as she could manage and threw her fingers to her chest. "I would be thrilled to watch you in action. Absolutely thrilled beyond measure if you think it's safe."

"Then you got it." He flipped the switch to roll the passenger window down. "I'll be collecting myself. Get me a weapon and get the kid ready."

"Yes, sir."

"There's one more thing, baby. Do you think you should take the boy with you?"

"Why not?"

"I mean, most of the men will be up here. What if they have a gun and… I can't imagine what they might do. Isn't it less risky for you, sugar, if we send the kid somewhere they can't find him?" She needed to get the boy away before they found the inevitable tracking device that would be hidden with the drugs.

"You're right. I love the way you think and want to take care of me." He kissed her, long and sloppily. She was so over being attracted to him. Definitely ready to talk in a normal strong voice that people listened to instead of rolling their eyes.

It took very little effort to get Rey out of the car and walking down the incline. It was as easy as dangling a carrot in front of a jackass.

The men she'd dealt with always liked their egos stroked along with other parts of their bodies. Easily manipulated without knowing they were controlled at all. She gave instructions to one of her men who left immediately with the boy. The brat would be kept in a safe place for later use. She couldn't risk the FBI swooping in with a last-minute rescue.

Soon, she was standing in the wing, watching Rey hike down a steep hill with two of his men. The valley was getting darker, but she could see him with the binoculars. He strutted across the field like absolutely nothing could go wrong.

She rolled down the window, crooking her finger toward her secret right-hand man. The shoes she'd bribed him with were on his feet—another item Rey had never questioned. His man had switched from roughneck work boots to Italian loafers and the man "in charge" had never asked why or how he could afford them.

"When we head back, move the boy to a secure location. Did you give the two men their instructions? They grab the bag and run without looking back."

"Yes, ma'am. They'll run like the devil's behind them. Or me."

She laughed. "I'll be free tonight. Stop by the house."

Zubict stood straight. She watched Zubict's crotch swell under the black jeans. He was an adequate lover. She could teach him a few ways to make the sex more enjoyable. Until the next man came into her sights.

Get a man to fall in love with your body and he'll do anything for you. She'd learned that lust was a powerful tool at a very early age.

"They dropped the bag and backed away. Our man is in place and has the shot," Zubict whispered over her shoulder.

"Take it."

Chapter Sixteen

Brandie heard the rifle shot at the same time she saw the impact of the bullet. The blood on Rey's chest was absorbed by his baby blue shirt, soaking into a larger and larger circle.

Rey was dead.

A look of surprise was forever locked on the dead man's face as he fell to his knees, creating two small puffs of dust she would never have noticed at another time. But she witnessed every nanosecond of his demise.

The puddle on his shirt got bigger and bigger as he fell. A dark red rip taking over the baby blue of the fabric like a sunset disappearing behind the Davis Mountains.

She was locked in place. Shots rang out around her, but she stood in the same spot staring, unblinking. Just like the open dead eyes of the man who had kidnapped her son. He stared at her from the ground. Eyes open wide. Mouth now full of West Texas dirt.

She'd never forget the dead man's look as his own men shot him in the back. It was the last thing he had expected.

"Come on!"

Mitch grabbed her arm to get her to move. It didn't work. Toby was with those murderers. She threw off his grip and ran toward the hills, heading straight toward the shooting.

"Are you crazy?" Mitch shouted. "We've got to get out of here!"

The man who had shot Rey could pick them off. She didn't know if it were easy for him to kill like that. Yet they were alive and the two men next to Rey were dead. She kept running toward the hills after the remaining man carrying the drugs. Faster. Watching the ground for anything that might trip her. She had to reach her son. Her vision blurred. She couldn't focus on the rocks or cactus or anything in her way. She just kept running.

Shots peppered the ground to her left.

"Brandie!" Mitch yelled.

More shots popped dirt into the air in front of them, causing her to shield her face and stop. Trying to protect her, Mitch pulled her into his chest, turning his back to their attackers.

"That's far enough," a woman's voice called from the top of the steep hill. "They won't miss again."

Whoever the woman was, she was still a long run away from where Brandie and Mitch had stopped. Far enough that her face was a blur next to the man clearly outlined holding a rifle. As tall as him, with blond hair past her shoulders that blew free in the breeze.

"Give me my son." Brandie heard her voice crack, already hoarse from screaming she hadn't heard. "We had a deal."

"Your deal is with a dead man."

Mitch laced his fingers with hers, tugging to get her to move. "We've got to get out of here."

"Not without Toby."

"You'll be contacted. I've got your number," the woman shouted, sounding smug. She disappeared behind a dark car.

Brandie collapsed to the ground. All of the fear she'd

been pushing away cut through her defenses and stabbed her heart. She'd failed. She couldn't go on. The last bit of light disappeared behind the mountaintops along with her last bit of hope.

Strong hands encircled her shoulders. She felt like a rag doll as Mitch lifted her into his arms and carried her. She cried into his denim jacket, unable to think, unable to stop.

"Stand up for me, sweetie." Mitch set her on her feet. "I've got to get my bearings and make a call."

She really tried to stand, but ended up in a pool on the ground. Face on top of her arms, the tears just kept coming. Then Mitch's voice cut through the fog. He was talking to someone.

"...to the southeast. Have you got a fix on the duffel?"

She turned her head enough to find him. He was using his cell, which shouldn't have been working. No one had reception out here.

"Roger that," the voice on the other end answered through the speaker. "Are you in need of emergency evac?"

Mitch looked all around them. "Negative. Will return on our own."

Brandie lifted herself to her elbows, then to her hands and knees before standing just behind the man she'd trusted with her son. They were surrounded by stars and darkness. Her eyes had already adjusted and she could see the brush and outlines of prickly pear. What she couldn't see was his black heart of betrayal.

"You lied to me."

"I had a backup plan."

"I told you to play this out by their rules, their instructions to the letter. That's what I said and that's what I meant. What part of our instructions said to put a tracking device in with the drugs?"

"Rangers are moving in and might have Toby back any

minute. That's what you want. That's what's most important, right? Nothing we did caused King's death or some crazy witch taking—"

"Do you know who has Toby?"

When Rey had her son, she'd been worried and scared. But she'd known he'd keep his word. Or she'd wanted to believe it so badly, she hadn't let herself believe anything else. This was different. They didn't know who had her sweet little boy. It was more real somehow.

"The car's over there. I marked it with my GPS." He pointed, looking at his glowing phone. They walked in silence. She prayed for his cell to buzz good news letting them know Toby was safe.

By the time they sat in the front seat, she knew the Rangers had been unable to rescue him. There was nothing to do this time other than wait. They had given up their leverage when Rey's men had disappeared with the cocaine.

Toby was truly kidnapped.

"Why did they keep him? Are they the same group? Did Rey's men kill their boss just to get him out of the way? What could they want us to do now?"

"I don't know, Brandie."

He started the engine, driving them back to Marfa on the long, deserted road. His cell still hadn't rung. At the stop sign, she put her hand on top of his.

"I know they didn't find Toby."

He shook his head, lips smashed flat into a straight line, frowning with his brows just as straight. "I can call to see what happened."

"He's gone. I assume they would have let you know if something had gone wrong. Or if they'd found him."

"I'm pretty sure Cord would have. He was there."

"I see. Would you take me home now?"

He squeezed her hand, and she didn't react. Ten more

minutes and they were at her home. Her parents' car was still in the driveway along with two Presidio County vehicles.

He parked his car, and she stopped him after he cracked his door open. With the dash lights on, she got a good look at his worried, anxious expression. It didn't matter. She'd made up her mind.

"I know I couldn't have done any of this without your help, Mitch. I wouldn't have found the drugs. I'm not even sure I could have pulled myself together to deliver a million dollars' worth of cocaine to drug dealers. But as much as I appreciate your help, you need to stay away from me."

"I don't understand."

Swirling beams shooting Christmas tree colors across her humble home pulled up behind them. The sheriff had arrived. The lights bounced around the neighborhood and off the rearview mirror, blinding her a bit. But she looked at Mitch, her heart more than a little broken at how he'd disregarded her feelings.

"It's not just you. I'm telling Pete the same thing. And if Cord comes around, he'll be next."

"You're in shock or something. You can't send all of us away. You need us to get Toby back."

"You're the reason he's gone!" she shouted, unable to control herself. Stopping. She laced her fingers together to stop the nervous habit of twisting whatever material was available around her finger. She wouldn't be calm until Toby was safe and back in her arms.

"You need to rethink this."

She quickly stared at her hands instead of the confusion on his face. "I know I'm perfectly within my rights. I'm listening to the kidnappers. You already know I'll do anything they want in order to get Toby back. Kicking you all out will prove that."

"Okay, we'll get rid of the cops, but you can't do this by yourself, Brandie."

Pete tapped on her window, and she pushed open her door. "You okay?" he asked. "We need to ask you about what happened out there."

"I've got nothing to say." She pushed by him and ran up the steps. Her dad already had the door open. "Out!" she yelled at the deputies. "Everybody get out of my house."

Her father held open his arms, and she ran to them. No matter what, being held by family was a sure way to feel protected. She needed that. Her mother joined them, encasing her tight in another set of arms. They all cried in the one living room corner free of gadgets.

She cried until she couldn't stand any longer. Her parents helped her to the couch. When she looked up, the three men she wanted to see the least stood in front of her. Almost identical in stature and mannerisms with their arms crossed.

"You aren't going to change my mind."

"You need everybody working on your side. Don't send us away." Mitch stood in the middle. His eyes looked a few years younger, but they also seemed a lot angrier.

She looked straight at him, hoping she could match his anger even with her eyes puffy. "You broke your word to me. You promised you'd do things my way without their help. Trackers, Rangers following them. They knew. They shot Rey."

"I kept my word. No one knew until the last minute. I already had everything I needed and let them know the tracking frequency through a secure email." Mitch took a step forward. Each arm was locked in the grip of the lawmen on either side of him, preventing his advancement.

"What's going on here?" her dad asked. Her mom

was as silent as ever, but still had her arms protectively around Brandie.

"Mitch is—"

"Wait," Cord cut her off. He turned to the deputies who had been monitoring for a ransom phone call. "Give us the room." Once they'd gone outside and the Ranger had shut the door he said, "There are three people other than our captain who know Mitch is undercover."

"What?" her parents asked together.

"Mitch is an undercover Texas Ranger," Brandie said with a little too much glee in her voice. She was proud of his hidden occupation, even if she didn't want him around any longer. The surprised look on her father's face seemed like vindication somehow. He was far from an authority on people and it gave her a spark of happiness that he had to rethink his opinions about her mechanic.

"Did they do something that caused Toby not to be released?" her mom said quietly. "Pete came and told us where you were. Is that why you don't want them here?"

"Yes."

"No."

Mitch had answered at the same time. Her mother looked at her, another tear fell from the corner of her eye. "Bud, get them out of here, please."

Her father stood, pointing to the door.

"This is a mistake," Mitch said again. "I can help. They can't know—"

"Get your stuff out of the garage. Lock the keys inside."

"Brandie?"

She made the mistake of looking into his pleading eyes as the other men physically hauled him from the house. She covered her face, replacing the memory of his pleading look with Rey's death stare. She'd never let that happen to Toby. Never!

Chapter Seventeen

"Hand over the impact wrench." Mitch used a low, threatening voice, but he didn't think the sheriff was listening.

"The owner instructed you to collect your things and lock the place up. I have to make sure that happens." But Pete slapped the wrench into Mitch's palm, then turned to Cord. "I assume you'll be watching Brandie and her parents. You'll keep me in the loop?"

"As much as I'm allowed."

"I'm. Not. Leaving." Mitch stated each word, securing a screw into the steel plates between each. The garage floor was safe to walk on again. He finished with more determination to retrieve Toby unharmed.

The look of disappointment on Brandie's face had cut him as surely as any blade.

"You've been ordered to return to Austin for reassignment." Cord pushed his worn Stetson off the back of his head with one hand and clawed at his hair with the other.

Mitch stowed the tools he'd been using. He ignored his two escorts and picked up parts lying on the garage floor from the break-in, stacking them on the shelves. It bugged him to see his garage in such a sloppy state.

Several boxes later it hit him that he thought of this place as his. That was, his and Brandie's. He clutched an air filter in his right hand and grabbed the metal shelving with his left trying not to fall as the enormity of the situation hit him.

The pain in his chest was from holding his breath. The pain in his jaw was from gritting his teeth. The blurring of his vision couldn't be from his eyes watering. He dropped the box and used the back of his sleeve to wipe his face.

A friendly couple of slaps on his back got a regular beat back to his aching heart. Toby was kidnapped.

"There's not a damn thing I can do," he mumbled. "I never thought he'd…"

The emotion crushing down on him like a vise was more than an undercover Ranger should feel. It was more than a friend felt for someone's missing child. That instance was full of the realization that Brandie and her son meant more to him than anything else.

And just like Brandie, he was willing to do anything to get him back. He'd fight to stay in Marfa. Even knowing that Brandie would never forgive him, he knew he had to stay.

"Look, man—" Cord's voice was full of empathy "—we've both been where you're at. Pete, you should know that my source who helped find your fiancée was Mitch."

"When those bastards took Andrea, I thought I'd go insane before I found her. Can't imagine it being a kid."

"You know we'll find Toby," Cord said.

Mitch clapped his arm on his superior's shoulder, locking gazes with him. "Get me reassigned here. I need to see this through."

Cord shook his head. "There's nothing I can do. Your work on the border is too important."

"Then I resign."

"You don't want to do that," Cord said.

Mitch caught Pete's uncharacteristic tension with his peripheral vision as the sheriff paced behind them. Would he have to fight both of them off to get back to Brandie? Or would they bend the rules to get back her son?

"I don't have a choice. I have to get Toby back."

IF HER FATHER didn't find something to occupy his time now that the deputies were gone, she might have to go stay at the café by herself. Every few minutes he had another question about Mitch that she didn't know the answer to—or at least she knew very few truths about him.

Once she'd convinced him that she'd only known since the night Rey's men had come to his house, her father withdrew to the kitchen to bother her mom awhile.

Brandie watched her mother fold the last of Toby's clothes and stack them in the laundry basket. The house was spotless. That's what her mother had been doing while waiting. Cleaning, cleaning and cleaning some more.

Now they were all back in her tiny living room wondering what to do. Brandie kept activating her cell screen, expecting a call any minute. She tried to convince herself it was the mystery woman she wanted to hear, but that wasn't the truth. She wanted Mitch to be on the other end.

She'd brought up his face several times on her screen and was one swipe away from asking him to come back. "What do I know about kidnappers or getting Toby back? This is all my fault. I can't think straight long enough to figure out how to fix it."

"I'm sorry, Brandie." Her father's voice was extremely soft, but it wasn't her imagination.

Her mother stopped smoothing Toby's clothes and stared at the other end of the couch where he sat. "What are you sorry for, Bud? You've been sorry a long time and need to actually tell her what you're sorry about."

Her dad's Adam's apple bobbed up and down in his wrinkled neck. "I should never have treated you like I did,

Brandie. I was so scared for you when you came home from college. We had such hopes that you'd get out of this little town and do something big with your life."

So had she. For five years he'd blamed her for ruining her life. And now? Why talk about it now?

"At first I was scared people would treat you bad. Then when Toby was born, I was afraid of how they'd treat my fatherless grandson. I wanted everybody to be as proud of him as I was. That's why I started making up stories about his father being a war hero. Can you forgive me?"

"I understood, Dad. I knew I disappointed you."

He knelt by the old rocker, taking her hand in his. "Honey, you've never been a disappointment. Never. You're a hardworking, kind and caring young woman. You're more than an old fart like me deserves."

Her father had always been a man of few words. Other than instructions on how to run the café and garage, this was the longest he'd spoken to her at one time in years. She knew how hard apologizing was for him, so she leaned forward and hugged his neck.

She'd loved him in spite of the hard words he'd said over the past few years. Part of being a family was loving each other no matter what. Both her parents had taught her that. It was something she lived by. A way of life that had kept her going no matter how ugly life got.

Soon they were all in another family hug. She felt happy, frightened, loved yet alone all at the same time. She realized her cell had slid from her lap to the floor when it began vibrating. Her mother picked it up and answered.

"Yes?"

Brandie could make out a deep voice, but not words. She stuck out her hand, but her mother shook her head and continued the conversation.

"That would be fine. We'd appreciate that." She disconnected. "Mitch offered to bring hamburgers from the DQ."

"I don't think that's a good idea."

"I didn't feel like cooking, so I agreed. I'll keep this—" she pocketed Brandie's phone "—so you can't call and cancel our dinner. I'm quite hungry." She lifted the laundry basket to her hip and moved into the short hallway.

"But Mom—"

"Let her go. This is the way she copes."

"Dad, Mitch will try to talk us into doing things his way. And his way involves law enforcement. I have to do whatever the kidnappers say."

"Then we won't let him stay. But like your mother, I haven't eaten and I'm beginning to feel kind of peckish. A burger sounds good while we're waiting." He winked, then followed her mom to Toby's room.

Waiting for Mitch to pull into the driveway didn't make her anxious. She was relieved for the very reason the talk with her dad had begun. She didn't know what to do. And she didn't know how she'd wait not doing anything at all.

Confused and conflicted. She wished she had someone to talk everything over with, but Mitch had become her best friend. Sadie worked with her almost every morning but they weren't close. Her high-school girlfriends had moved. And she hadn't been in college long enough to make lasting friendships.

She'd grown more dependent on Mitch the past six months than she'd realized. And that's why she felt alone. She recognized the sound of his car's engine a short time later. Prepared to tell him to leave as soon as she said thanks for the burgers, she stood in the middle of the room, ready for his knock.

"Come on in," she called out.

The door opened, and he extended his arm through. His

hand held two white sacks. "I didn't have a white flag. You ready to discuss a truce?"

Unable to send him away again, she took one of the sacks and walked it to her son's room. She wanted to cry, but held herself together as her dad took two burgers and proclaimed they were fine where they were.

Brandie had to face him. Her stomach growled at the smell of mustard and onions. She didn't want to be hungry while her son wasn't home, but she hadn't really eaten all day and needed the fuel to function.

Mitch had pulled the burgers out onto the table and opened two bottles of water. "Mind if I join you?"

"Go ahead and sit." Brandie forced every bite down, hoping she wouldn't be sick.

They ate in silence. Then he waved a napkin. "I should have thought of this when I came inside. I didn't know if Bud would have his shotgun ready or not."

"I think Pete took it this morning so he wouldn't accidently shoot someone. I guess if they'd contacted you or you had any news you would have told me when you got here. Right?"

"I would have called you. I wouldn't have waited."

"Was Pete civil when you got your stuff from the garage? Dad asked him to follow you and make sure you left."

"Yeah. But I didn't get anything except a change of clothes and my toothbrush. Everything's locked tight. Alarm's on." He finished his last French fry and licked the salt from his fingers. He must have caught the way she was looking at him because he arched those normally very straight brows.

"Did I really have to say you're fired?"

"Well, that is what I came to talk to you about. See, I sort of quit."

"You can call it anything you want. Hand over my keys." She stood with her hand out, waiting.

"No. Wait. I mean that I resigned from the Texas Rangers. If you still need a mechanic…"

"Why?" she asked, plopping back onto the hard wooden chair.

"I knew you wouldn't keep me around if I didn't."

"But Mitch—"

"We need to find Toby. I can help. I can't if they send me back to Austin." He sat back, crossed his arms, looking firm in his decision to end his career in order to find her son.

"Thank you." He was right. She couldn't think beyond finding Toby. "Where do we start?"

"We wait for a call. In the meantime, we go back to the beginning and see how all these events mesh together. They have to have something in common or be some kind of pattern."

"What if it's days before the woman on the hill calls?"

"Then we'll have longer to think this through, maybe figure out who she is. King couldn't have that many associates. With or without your permission, Cord and Pete are still working on Toby's case. They just aren't working with us."

"Am I wrong? I don't think they'll contact me if they see deputies hanging around the house. I just want him home safe and sound." She just couldn't imagine what might be going through his young mind. "He'll probably toss a fit if he can't take his big boy shower before he goes to bed."

"Big boy? I haven't heard about that."

"Mom was at choir practice when he spent the night a couple of months ago. Dad didn't want to bathe Toby, so he taught him how to take a shower. That's what he's done every night since."

"I don't think he'll get his shower, but I don't think he's being mistreated. King was a blowhard." He gathered the paper and ketchup containers pushing them back into the sack, then tossing it into the waste bin like any man would.

Such an ordinary thing.

"Toby loves you," he said. "He's not going to blame you for this. We'll get him back and he'll be fine."

"I hope you're right, Mitch. I'll never forgive myself if he doesn't come home."

"Neither will I."

Chapter Eighteen

Zubict waltzed through the front door using a key. His audacity made Patrice want to shoot him. Unfortunately, she needed him and would have to play along with his imaginary importance.

"The child is where we discussed?" she asked.

"Of course. Kid cried the whole way. I hope that woman has better luck with him than me. Does Rey got two large sitting under the mattress? She was more expensive than you said."

"I think I can handle a reimbursement. I've made a list of things you should take care of— What are you doing?"

He slipped the last button through its hole. "Taking off my shirt. What's it look like? I figured you'd want some of this." He flexed his slender muscles.

"We have things to do. There's time for that later." She brushed him aside and crossed the room for her notepad. If it weren't for sex the men she knew would have no reason to accomplish anything.

"Hey, ain't you afraid the cops will be showing up here?"

"Why?"

"Rey's dead." He used an incredulous expression as if she were the dumb one.

But she wasn't. She'd convinced Rey to put everything

in her name several years ago. "This is my house. No one can trace anything back to me through him." She extended her hand. "You should give me his set of keys."

"Why should I do that?" He shrugged, letting his shirt fall to the carpet.

"Zubict, I could use your assistance." She reached into her handbag on the counter, removing Rey's gift to her. Rey's new Glock 21 .45 ACP was heavier in her hand than she remembered. "But I will shoot you between the eyes if you don't put your shirt back on and give me the keys to my house."

"You are some real piece of work," he said as he followed her instructions.

"Yes, I am. You'll get your cash back when I say you'll get it." She watched him as he tucked the shirt back into his pants. "Let's get on with things, shall we?"

"Your wish is my command."

"Are you familiar with decoys? You are my decoy. While you're in San Angelo, I'll be setting us up a huge score. Bigger than anything I've moved this past year."

"You mean the Chessmen has moved. What you's got to do with it? Rey said we worked for the Chessmen."

"Think whatever you want, Zubict." She flipped her hair over her shoulder and tapped her nails on the counter next to the handgun. "I've made all the arrangements and have a job for you tonight."

Her suppliers had taken notice of her accomplishments. She didn't need the praise of the pawn in front of her. She handed him a piece of paper, ready for his role in this game to end.

"Take the trunk of cocaine to this address in San Angelo."

"That's gonna take me hours. I won't get back 'til late

tomorrow." He whined. "You's sure ya can live without me that long?"

"Believe me, I'll make do." His whining reminded her of the character she'd played for Mr. Rook. She loved the burnt orange leather skirt she'd worn. Just watching the games of chess he played improved her game. It would have been fun to pit herself against him. Then again, she had a much riskier game that she'd won—considering he was awaiting trial. Another loose end she'd tucked away.

"How much we chargin' for the bag?" he asked, crossing the room and dropping the strap on his shoulder.

"Nothing. We're returning it. No lip or I'll—"

"Right. I gotcha. Take it. Drop it off. Come back here. No problem."

"Great. Once you do that, we'll be ready for the shipment from Mexico."

"And I suppose you's got it all figured out and don't need no help. So what's in it for me?"

"I chose you over Rey. You know what you'll get when this is over." She pulled his face to hers and kissed him until she felt him harden against her. "Business before pleasure, darling."

"That's right. You just wait until I get back." He staggered backward when she released the sides of his face. His slick-soled Italian loafers slid across the carpet, back farther until his hand found the knob. He left with a fool of a grin on his drooling face.

She turned the dead bolt. Zubict wouldn't be returning. The buyers in San Angelo had agreed to take care of that loose end for her.

The organization she'd been working with for the past year had offered her a position. She was leaving Alpine and West Texas for good. Leaving the dust, the emptiness, the morons who were Rey's friends and hit on her every time his back was turned.

This paltry little house was a shack compared to what she'd be living in next week. Just one thing was in her way. She glanced at the chessboard and the unfinished game that Rey had been playing against an unknown opponent.

Switching the CD player to her music, she twisted the knob as loud as her ears could stand it. The neighbors were far enough away and used to the loud bass reverb powering from her speakers. She reset the Civil War chess pieces on their squares. The silver-based pieces representing the south called to her. It was illogical—everyone knew that the south lost.

This time, in her game, they would definitely win. She removed three pieces from the north. After all, she'd removed them from her game board in real life. Just a few more details and everything would be perfect.

Now what had she done with that leather skirt and jacket?

Chapter Nineteen

"Why haven't they called?" Brandie chanted from the bed. She clasped her cell between her palms as if she were praying with it, then twisted the small blanket as she flipped to her other side.

Mitch watched her grow more upset as the sun rose higher in the sky. She hadn't slept and as a result of her staying awake, he'd been awake all night, as well. He wasn't taking any chances with her safety.

Not after that unknown witch on the mesa had shot King before he could say a word. One second the man opened his mouth to speak and the next he fell to the ground with a hole in his chest. Mitch didn't try to convince Brandie to leave her house for a safer venue. Nope, she needed to be close to her son's things. Even he could see that.

She'd curled up on Toby's bed, and he'd set his butt on a cushion with his back against the bedroom door. He faced the window, ready for an intruder. No one was getting to her and that included her parents who had stayed over and slept in Brandie's room. She didn't have to face anyone until she was ready.

If they hadn't already been awake, the texts and messages from Cord would have awakened him every hour. He'd ignored them all along with an occasional text from Pete asking for updates. He'd wait, talk things over with

Brandie and see if she wanted them in the loop. Or if she wanted their help.

At the moment the answer was a decisive no.

"Do you still have eggs in the fridge? Since we're up, might as well make breakfast."

She rolled over to face him, one of Toby's stuffed dinosaurs in her arms. "Mom and Dad get up early. They'll take care of things."

"You ready to get up, then?"

"No. Not yet." Her eyes slowly dropped to a half-closed position, then all the way shut.

He took out his cell, responding once to each lawman that he'd get back with them later. He wanted a notepad and pen because something important was at the edge of his memory. There was something about this puzzle that he couldn't piece together. If he wrote down what he could remember from the case files, maybe he could put questions together that Brandie could answer or allow him to ask Cord about.

"Aren't you tired?" Her words were mumbled into the fuzzy brontosaurus. "You could squeeze in behind me if you want to stretch out."

"I'm fine." He'd be curled much too close to her on that junior-size bed.

"Oh." She shifted closer to the edge next to the wall.

"There's no way I'll fit on that short bed."

"Okay. It was just a thought. Might have been nice."

"Do you want me to hold you?" He was surprised. Totally willing and very surprised. Wait. No way. He was staying put. Not that he couldn't use a few minutes of shut-eye. But Bud Quinn was on the other side of that wall and could come into this room at any moment wanting an update.

"It's probably safer to stay where we are," she whispered.

Bud might have apologized to his daughter, but he still had a hot temper and didn't need to be provoked. Mitch stayed exactly where he was, satisfied that Brandie had thought him holding her would be nice.

They'd get Toby back and send her parents to their own home. Then he'd hold her exactly how he wanted. And that would be skin to silky skin. It wouldn't happen straight away, but when things were back to normal…it wouldn't take long.

He rubbed his eyes, attempting to get the image of a naked Brandie out of his head. It just got more vivid. He needed to think about the case.

First objective—get Toby back. Then figure out how to tell the spitfire hugging a stuffed green fur ball that he was head over heels in love with her.

Yep. One-hundred-percent in love. It was the only thing that explained his actions. Toby might have a daddy crush, as Cord put it, but Mitch definitely had a sexy Brandie crush.

"How long have you been a Ranger?"

He looked up from his phone into her brilliant wide-awake blue eyes. "Just under three years. Almost all that time has been undercover. I was a state trooper before that. And four years with the Austin PD narcotics unit—I joined the force straight out of junior college."

"I don't know anything about you. As often as I wanted to know, I never asked before. I didn't consider it any of my business. Do you have family?"

"No brothers or sisters. My mom and dad are still around. But they split when I was young. They also fight a lot and it makes it easy to avoid them." Real easy after years of practice.

"So where did you go for Christmas? Did you spend it with friends? When you left for that week, I didn't really think you'd be back." Brandie squished the stuffed toy closer to her breasts.

"I said I would be, but I get it." He had a sudden urge to be a stuffed brontosaurus. "I haven't kept up with many friends. They do most of their talking through social media and in my line of work, that could get me killed."

"So where did you disappear to then?"

"A hellish week of training in Austin. Didn't sleep a wink on that soft hotel bed. Two months on that army cot in the garage and I'm spoiled for life."

"Was it the cot or the smell of grease? So no permanent address?" She smiled softly.

How she could still have a normal conversation with what she'd been through in the past couple of days was beyond his understanding. But that was one of the things he loved about her. One of the reasons he was in love period. He'd never met anyone like her.

"Nope. This is the longest I've been in one spot since I stopped wearing a trooper uniform."

"Do you like it here?"

He liked her. Would go anywhere she wanted to go. Take her and Toby away, or find a quiet, safe place to stay here in Marfa. "Very much."

"You look surprised."

"I sort of am." Now wasn't the time to explain just how surprised he was that he'd fallen in love. "I grew up in the city. But these last three years working in smaller towns has been okay. I like the people here in Marfa. For all the turmoil behind the scenes, it's pretty quiet. Working on a car wins every time if put up against being undercover with dope dealers. I like the challenge of finding the problem and fixing it."

"Did you really walk away from your job last night?"

"Let's just say that I didn't gain any points by not reporting back to headquarters."

She swung her legs over the edge of Toby's dinosaur bedspread. She began to say something several times. Indecisive wasn't her norm. "I, um, need to tell you about Toby's dad. His name was Private Tobias Ryland."

"Okay." Not that it mattered to him. It had never mattered.

"You see, we weren't serious or anything. In fact, we'd only gone on a couple of dates while he was visiting one of his friends in Alpine. I told him I was pregnant after he returned to Fort Hood. His unit shipped out soon after. He was supposed to have added us to his will and stuff like that. Guess he didn't get around to it."

"Did you contact the military? How did you find out he was…dead?"

"His best friend in Alpine called me. I was already back here by then." She paused, smiling with the slightest upturn of her lips. "Thank you, Mitch. I don't have many friends. You coming back to help, well, it just means the world to me."

She stood and put a hand out to help him to his feet.

"I couldn't run back to Austin."

She completely caught him off guard with the kiss. Her hands caught his cheeks and brought his lips to hers, holding him in place. Why his hands cupped her slender fingers against his stubble instead of wrapping around her body, he'd never know. Sooner than he wanted, it was over and she was sinking back to the pads of her feet from her tiptoes.

"Thank you for coming back. I can't ask you to go away and leave us. Toby needs your help." She dropped her arms against her jean-covered thighs. "I need your help. I wouldn't be able to get out of his bed if you weren't here."

"Of course you would." He hooked a strand of her gorgeous red hair behind her ear. "You're the strongest and bravest person I know, Brandie."

She dropped her head to his chest, wrapping her arms around his waist. "What are we going to do if they don't call, Mitch? What are we going to do?"

He tilted her chin back so he could look into her eyes, which were filled with tears again. "We won't stop looking. We'll bring him home. Don't doubt me, Brandie. We will find him."

She stepped back, shoving her hair out of her face, and blew out a long breath. "Tell me how long we wait. *You* make that decision. Do you think we need to bring Pete and Cord back? Just tell me what to do and don't make me decide. It's too hard to think."

"I can do that." Convincing her parents that he was capable of making decisions might be another story. "But to be honest, Pete and Cord didn't stop because you told them to. They're still looking. Ready to get started?"

"I'm going to grab a quick shower before I face my parents."

"I'm grabbing coffee."

The smell of bacon and eggs filled his nostrils. He was a lot hungrier than he wanted to admit.

Olivia was in the kitchen, her apron on top of her clothes. She'd made a breakfast casserole and was scooping out the first spoonful for Bud.

"Good morning, Mitch. I can fix you regular eggs if you prefer them."

"Is that the recipe they serve at the café?"

"Sure is."

"I can't get enough of that stuff. Load me up with as much as you can spare."

"You're a lucky young buck not having to worry about cholesterol." Bud forked a bite into his mouth. "No real bacon. No fried eggs. How'd you sleep?"

Brandie's father didn't pause between bites or questions.

"I didn't, sir."

Olivia set his plate in front of him along with a large cup of coffee.

"That going to be good for my daughter if you're called into action today when you find my grandson?" Bud set the fork down and crossed his arms on the edge of the table, leaning forward.

Mitch could finally see through the rough edges. Bud Quinn's eyes were just as puffy as Olivia's. They'd been crying. They were worried and scared. Everybody was doing the best they could.

"I've gone without sleep before. I give you my word that I'll bring Toby home."

"I'm going to hold you to that, son."

"So am I, sir."

He'd finished half his plate when Brandie joined them wearing the worn jeans he loved. The old T-shirt was worn through in places but she had a tank on under it. Bud harrumphed, letting Mitch know that he'd seen the way he'd looked at his daughter.

"Are you really going to wear that, sweetheart?" her mom asked. "What if someone stops by?"

"Don't worry, Momma. I'll be working at the café getting it cleaned up. I'll go nuts if I just sit here waiting."

"We'll hold down the fort here, then," she announced.

"You ready?" Brandie asked.

The last bite went into his mouth, he gulped the last sip of coffee and they were soon climbing into his car.

He shifted into gear and teased, "So much for me making the decisions."

Chapter Twenty

The cleaning was going well. Most of the broken stuff was in a pile at the back of the garage. Two hours of physical labor and no sleep had Brandie ready for a nap.

"I have no idea how I'm going to work repairs into the budget." She barely got the words out before a yawn overtook her.

"I can help."

"Oh, no. Dad and I will figure it out with the insurance company." She picked some of the glass pieces out of the jukebox. It crushed her heart to lose this antique. "Did I ever tell you that this jukebox is how my dad first spoke with my mom? She was looking at the songs and he asked her if she liked traditional rock or country."

"I wonder if someone can restore it?"

"Oh, I can't afford that. You know we're barely treading water around here. I have to get this place open again soon or there's no reason to try." She sat in a clean booth, suddenly so tired she could barely move.

"Why don't you lie down awhile?"

"There's so much to do. And what if that woman calls?"

She checked the volume on her cell again to verify she hadn't switched it to vibrate or mute. It was as loud as it would go. The background picture of Toby with his favorite dinosaur made her choke up. She wouldn't cry again. She didn't have the strength.

"Don't worry, I'll wake you up." Mitch scooped her from the vinyl seat and carried her to his comfy cot.

The lack of sleep had definitely caught up with her. Her arms were too heavy to lift. She barely got one crooked under her head before the faint sounds from the café faded into complete silence.

Brandie woke with a start. Voices—lots of them—broke into her dream of pushing Toby on his swing in the backyard. In the dream she'd gone from laughing with her son to having her numb hands tied to the posts. Fighting the pins and needles shooting through her arm, she pushed herself to a sitting position, her arm waking from sleep a second later. She recognized those voices.

"Why's he being so stubborn? He's put his entire career at risk. Does he plan on confronting the kidnappers alone?" Cord answered from inside the café.

"They wouldn't be here if they'd heard from the kidnappers. Any word on the missing drugs?" Pete asked.

"Never even found the device Mitch put inside the duffel lining."

"Did you try tracking them the old-fashioned way?" Nick Burke's voice was as quiet as usual, but she knew what they were talking about. Toby's abductors.

"Hey, you're awake," the sheriff said from the doorway. "Mitch, Brandie's awake."

There was no way to avoid it. She'd given him permission, and Mitch had taken charge. He'd brought the law back on to the case. She had enjoyed the couple of hours of peace they'd had. Even if she'd been worried out of her mind. There would be no getting rid of these guys. Facing the kidnappers alone would be even harder.

"Feel better?" Mitch squeezed past Cord, Pete and Nick.

"I told them to wait to move the jukebox. And for the record, there's no news about Toby."

"What are they doing?"

His hair was wet, still dripping enough to dampen his collar. He'd finally showered—he hadn't had time when she'd left the house so quickly and he'd refused to take one here if she was alone.

"They thought it was easier to move the jukebox out through the garage for the guy to pick it up. Andrea found a restorer willing to take it. I didn't think you'd want it to just hit the landfill. Looks like it's going to get stuck to me."

"That's fantastic, but I meant what are they all doing here?" She answered positively, even though it broke her heart to part with the antique. "Did you say Andrea?"

"Yeah. I was surprised. Your friends came to help clean up and get the place open again." He grabbed her hand, excited for once with a smile as big as a canyon.

She jerked him to a stop and whispered, "Mitch, I can't do this now. I don't think I can pretend that nothing's wrong."

"Your *friends* don't expect you to fake anything. They're here to help. Period."

Friends?

They went through the doorway and met a small crowd. Nick Burke and his fiancée, Beth Conrad, stood near the kitchen. Pete and his fiancée, Andrea Allen, were at the counter. Cord was just inside the door looking at his wife, Kate, who sat in a booth with their son.

"We wanted to help clean up, Brandie," said Andrea.

"I hope you don't mind us just barging in." Kate lifted Danver into her arms.

"It's purely selfish on our part," Beth added. "We don't have anywhere to meet while the café is closed."

She was about to lose it. Fall apart. Her seams were coming undone because of their kindness.

"I really don't think this is a good—"

"No. Just say thank-you and let them help." Mitch squeezed her hand, wrapped tight within his own. "You said you wanted me to make some decisions for you. Well, this is the first. And if either of these guys try to talk to you about Toby, they'll have to answer to me."

"Right. I might. Just so I can knock some sense into you." Cord slowly threw a fake punch at Mitch.

"I forced Nick to leave his beloved cows for the afternoon. But seriously, Brandie. Just say the word and we'll head back to the ranch," Beth said.

"We're not here in a law enforcement capacity," Cord added. "We realize the kidnapper might not see it that way. We've canvassed six blocks and made certain it was clear."

"We just couldn't stand you facing all this alone," Andrea said.

A quick look around the room showed her how valuable their help had already been. Everything was in order, but the friendship they were offering meant so much more. "Please stay. I'll see if I can get some food together."

"Oh, no, you don't." Andrea dashed to her side and gently tugged her to Kate's booth. "We're taking care of food and cleanup. You just sit down and don't worry about a thing. Maybe you can play with Danver so Kate can help me finish the storage room."

Friends.

Mitch slid into the booth next to her, leaning on the table, that grin still on his face. "You're surprised."

"To say the least." She raised her voice so they could all hear her. "I can't say thank-you enough."

"It's the least we can do. We love this place as much as we love you, Brandie." Kate put her son back in his seat.

The memories of Toby at that age swept her back. He'd spent most of his days in a playpen or swinging chair until he'd turned four and started at the day care.

"Oh, yeah, Sadie stopped by." Mitch's smile disappeared. "She said she was here to help, but she sure wasn't dressed for it. Took off when Andrea and Pete pulled up, but she left you a note. It's in the garage office."

He seemed relieved that she hadn't stayed. Come to think of it, at times he'd gone out of his way to avoid Sadie.

"Is that who that was? I thought there was something familiar about her," Beth said through the service window in the kitchen. "I saw those expensive heels and leather skirt and just didn't think of your waitress."

Kate tapped her bright pink nails on the table. "That's weird. I recognized her wig, but the way she was dressed, it never clicked the woman was Sadie."

"Wig?" the people in the room asked together.

Kate looked up, surprised everyone didn't have that piece of information stored in their brain. "You guys really never noticed? It's a very good wig, but it slipped one afternoon a couple of weeks ago. From my angle in the booth I could see her real hair sticking out around her neck."

"How could I have missed a wig? All this West Texas dust has clogged up my detective skills." Beth laughed at her own joke.

Everybody knew she was the DEA's representative in West Texas. She and Pete had both been abducted into Mexico just before Christmas. Mitch moved over to talk with the men and the women gleefully joined her in the booth.

"Like I said, it was a really good wig. But her hair's a beautiful color so I have no idea why she wears it," Kate said quietly.

"Well, I wouldn't know." Andrea played with her multiple necklaces. "She avoids me like the plague. Pete teased that she was afraid of mouthy women."

They all laughed, but Brandie kept her head down, trying to avoid the conversation. She'd seen Sadie without the wig and didn't know if her waitress would want so many people knowing, especially the county sheriff.

"Brandie, you look as guilty as sin. You already knew about the wig, didn't you? Do you know why she wears it?" Andrea asked bluntly, which was her way.

"I shouldn't say anything. It's sort of private."

"Was it breast cancer?" Kate asked.

"That was the first thing I thought until I saw how long her hair was. She told me she had a violent ex-boyfriend." Brandie lowered her voice. It somehow made it feel less gossipy to talk about Sadie if all the guys couldn't hear.

"Oh, my, a waitress in hiding with a mysterious backstory. I'm intrigued." Andrea whispered, too.

The men cleared a path for the jukebox. They joked like it was a normal day. But it wasn't. Their body language was sharp and on edge. Tensions were high waiting on a call that may or may not come.

"Did she mention anything else?" Andrea nudged her in the side.

"Just that she needed the extra money."

"If I knew the tips were that good here, I would have taken a job months ago. That was a real leather jacket and skirt. Not to mention the matching Louis Vuitton bag and shoes." Beth looked around the booth at their questioning faces. "What? I happen to like expensive shoes."

"They were probably knockoffs, right? You can't be certain they were the real thing." Brandie had a hard time believing Sadie had been dressed so nicely. "She was constantly suggesting I take off early so she could close up the café and get a couple of extra tips. Why would she work here if she didn't need the money?"

The three other women looked directly at Mitch who was helping maneuver the jukebox through the door. His lean muscles bulged as he lifted and pushed. He caught her stare and winked at her.

"She didn't stand a chance even in that burnt-orange outfit." Beth leaned across the table to pat Brandie's hand. "The only person he ever smiles for is you. And honey, I was a foot model. Those shoes were the real deal."

"Wait a minute. Beth, are you sure about that color?" Andrea asked.

"Very sure. It was exactly the shade of your college hoodie, Kate. I wouldn't have noticed if she hadn't been wearing those studded rolling boots. They're sixteen-hundred-dollar shoes." Beth twisted her long black hair around her finger. "Whoever that violent ex-boyfriend was he certainly had money."

"It can't be possible." Andrea grabbed Brandie's hand, gripping it anxiously. "Was Sadie's real hair color platinum-blond?"

"Yes."

"Pete! Oh, my gosh! Pete get in here!" Andrea jumped up from the table, impatient for the sheriff to return. "I think she's that woman who was working with Rook the night he tried to blackmail my dad."

Brandie's heart latched on to the hope that the nightmare might actually be over soon.

MITCH JUMPED BACK into the café with his heart racing. He hadn't heard a cell ring, but he was certain something had happened. Brandie was as white as a sheet.

"Do you have an address for Sadie, and her last name?" Andrea asked.

"I think she said she lives in Alpine, but it would be on her application," Mitch answered, not understanding why they wanted to know about Sadie.

"What's the matter?" Pete asked, finally pushing past the jukebox.

"Remember that blonde I described who was taking orders from Rook? It's Sadie. At least I think she's the same chick." Andrea was as excited as a little kid on their birthday.

"You said she had long blond hair," the sheriff said.

"She does. That's what we were just talking about. Sadie has long blond hair. That's the reason she never waited on me. She knew I could identify her." Andrea noticed Brandie's shaking hands and slid back into the booth.

"There was a tall blonde woman at Bishop's place," Nick added from the garage.

"The woman who took Toby stood just as tall as Zubict on that ridge. That would make her at least five-ten or eleven. It sure looked like she was a blonde." Mitch couldn't believe it.

"Sadie's about that tall with the shoes she wears," Brandie whispered, but everyone was quiet enough to hear her.

"Give me her address and I'll get the local PD to bring her in for questioning," Cord said to Mitch as he came into the café.

Mitch knew where the employee records were. It was a good thing Brandie didn't have to tell him since she looked like she was about to be sick. How could Sadie be involved in Toby's kidnapping or in Beth or Andrea's abductions and still be bold enough to wait tables on the very people she should be afraid of?

Mitch handed Cord the application, and the Ranger stepped out the front door to make the call. Mitch couldn't get to Brandie. Andrea had an arm around her shoulders. Exactly where he wanted to be.

"You really think it's possible that this woman was working with Jones, Lopez and Rey?" Pete asked.

"You mean Rook, Bishop and King," Mitch confirmed.

"Right. They used code names, but their fingerprints match them to the Mexican and FBI criminal database. Rey used both translations of his name. The arrogant bastard went by King King," Pete said.

"They're all chess pieces," Mitch mumbled.

"Both men had multiple chess boards at their haciendas. We know that Rook was working with a group, but he won't give up anything about them."

"She's been playing us all this time." Mitch hadn't been confronted with anything like this during his career. It was hard to conccive, harder to believe it was real.

"What do you mean?" Beth asked.

"She's been playing everybody, us, these chess men. But what's the most powerful playing piece in chess?"

"The Queen," the group answered.

"Sadie, or whatever her name is…" Brandie said with the barest breath. "She's been in charge all along. She considers herself the Queen."

Sadie's message. What had she said?

"Dammit, what did I do with the note she left? Office." He hit the counter with his palm and locked eyes with the man still on the garage side of the jukebox. "Nick, I tossed the envelope—a blue one like for a card—on top of the loose papers on the garage desk."

"Got it." He took off running.

Looking around the room of intelligent people they all seemed baffled, but no one thought his conclusion was wrong. No one argued a different possibility. They were all just waiting, like him.

Nick had opened the envelope. He handed the card across the jagged glass to Mitch using a work glove.

"It's a drawing. I think it's silos."

"That's it? She doesn't mention Toby? Or any exchange? Or demand what she wants? Are you sure there's nothing else in the envelope?" Brandie pulled her hair back, landing her hands around her neck. Cutting herself off from comforting gestures Andrea tried to offer.

"Sorry. Nothing."

"Show it to us," Brandie said. "I don't understand. Is that where Toby is?"

The women tried to calm her down. Cord took a picture with his cell, and Pete grabbed something to substitute for an evidence bag. Nick pulled while Mitch shoved at the stuck jukebox.

Mitch shoved harder. And harder again. Receiving a strange look from Nick when he threw up his hands and backed away.

"Hey, man. Maybe this isn't a good idea right now," Nick said. "You don't want to wreck it more."

"Dammit!" Mitch wanted to punch something. The anger and frustration he felt had nothing to do with a stuck antique. "We're not going to get a phone call. It's a riddle and if we're going to get Toby back, we have to solve it."

Chapter Twenty-One

"That was Alpine PD. No one matching Sadie's description lives at the address on her application. That would have been too easy. I had another message. Your man Gary Zubict was found dead from a drive-by in San Angelo." Cord closed his notebook and stuck it in his pocket.

Mitch had ducked out of the café to wait with Cord. The energy inside had gone from overly excited to flat and pensive. They all realized—especially Brandie—that knowing Sadie was involved didn't change the fact that the woman still had Toby.

"If she was taking care of loose ends like Zubict, why risk coming here? What was so important about this note that she had to deliver it herself?" Mitch was still baffled. The picture made no sense. "What the hell does she want with the kid?"

Cord looked past him, indicating the open door where Brandie stood.

"I want to know the answer to that myself," she said, standing next to him.

Mitch wrapped his arm around her shoulders, drawing her close to his side.

Brandie must have seen the way Cord shot his evil-eye warning. She pulled away to lean on the awning post, hands around the back of her neck, as tense as always.

"Silos in this country are few and far between. It will take us hours to check them all out." Brandie grabbed the drawing. "I don't know what to do."

Cord pulled out the notepad again. "Let's go with your theory, Mitch. If Sadie considers herself the Queen and smarter than us, then why did she set up all her men to fail? Hell, she had King shot in the back in front of you."

"It sounds like she's running the board. Taking out all the major pieces one at a time. She had us do it for her with Rook and Bishop. At each abduction we confiscated what we thought were major gun shipments. While we're dealing with one set of problems—"

"That's when we discover a second shipment heading across the border," Cord finished.

"Wherever she has us looking for Toby…"

"Yeah, you're right." Cord slapped him on the back, took out his cell and started dialing as he walked to his truck.

"What did you two just figure out?" Brandie asked.

"She's using the hunt for Toby as a distraction."

"Sure doesn't feel like a distraction."

"You called your parents? I'm surprised they're not here already."

"We convinced them there might be a message or phone call at home. But everyone knows there won't be." Her cell was still in her hand. "That picture. Does it seem kind of amateurish to you? As if it weren't thought out ahead of time?"

"Yeah, kind of last-minute, which doesn't match the profile of a meticulous planner." He reached for Brandie, but she paced in the opposite direction. "So maybe Toby's kidnapping isn't a part of her plan."

"I know how to find her." Beth burst through the

café door. "The shoes. We can track her by her sixteen-hundred-dollar shoes. There's got to be a record of a sale."

The buzz returned as they went back inside. He waited, holding the door for Brandie. He was just opening his mouth to tell her to ignore Cord when she placed a hand on his chest.

"I think we should put a little space between us. It's hard enough functioning with Toby gone. I can't handle the questions and the looks. Let's keep our focus on finding him. And I mean everyone's focus. Don't you think *we* can and should wait?" she whispered as the group got quiet.

"Sure." He agreed, wanting the exact opposite.

Brandie's whole existence was wrapped around what other people thought. She needed to think about herself and believe that her true friends would love her no matter what. But he'd respect her decision. He had no right not to. No matter what fantasy was in his head about their relationship.

"Pete, as much as I love you, sweetie, I can't do any research with that archaic computer system at the courthouse." Andrea gathered her things. "We'll be at the house where I have a very competent system and high-speed internet."

Brandie still stood around without a job. She absent-mindedly picked up a few things and made another pile of broken objects. She wanted answers, and everyone was trying to get them. The least she could do was appreciate all their assistance.

"Thanks for helping, Andrea. I'd be helpless researching on a computer." Brandie felt out of her element. Everyone was busy, but her best skill was running a café.

"I'm glad I learned something after three higher education degrees." She laughed and joined Pete. "I'll locate the silos and the future hubby over here will coordinate a search."

While Kate spoke in a low voice to Cord, Beth was hopelessly attempting to strap Danver into his seat.

"Here, let me get that." Brandie took pity on her, but secretly thanked her that she had something to occupy her hands.

"Thanks. I've been practicing and still can't get the hang of this thing. Nick will be the designated car seat guru in our household."

"Are you two…?" Brandie pointed to Danver.

"Oh, no, sorry. The wedding's planned for my mom and dad's summer break at the university. He wanted a short engagement, but I never imagined spring on a ranch could be so all consuming." She looped the diaper bag over her shoulder. "You ready to go?"

"I'm staying here. If they won't let me search for Toby, then I'm staying here."

"That's not what—"

"Right. But *I* decided to stay. I appreciate that everyone thinks I'll be safer there with you. But Sadie's not trying to kill me and if she wants to get in touch, I want to be close. I'll feel like I'm contributing."

Beth cupped her hands around Brandie's shoulders, the most sincere look on her face. "Then I'll stay here. Is that okay with you? I can do everything with Andrea by phone."

"Sadie pretended to be my friend while she was spying, learning our secrets and doing I don't know what. If she doesn't want anything from me then why hasn't she called? Do you think it's because you're all here? Maybe she still has someone watching us?"

"It's possible, but Pete has deputies patrolling close by.

They would have seen someone who doesn't belong in town," Beth said. "I'll stay, okay?"

"I'd cry my appreciation, but I don't have any more tears. They're all gone. I just know I'd go crazy forty-five minutes from town."

"That's okay. You're saving me. If I went with Kate and Andrea I'd be in tears, too. I think Nick asked her to show me how to change a diaper." She laughed.

Beth laughed a lot more now than when she'd first arrived in Marfa. She was good for Nick who seemed back to his old self after being shot over a year ago. Andrea and Pete were good together. Kate and Cord were icons. She wanted that type of love.

The real kind that took in each other's strengths and weaknesses. Her mom and dad loved each other, but it was totally different from what these three couples had.

Mitch looked her direction. She needed to tell him she wasn't leaving. He'd be upset and want to stay. *So let him.* Her inner voice was telling her she deserved him and all the comfort that he brought her. But Toby deserved his skill.

"Everyone knows what to do?" Cord asked. "Pete will handle all the coordination. His deputies are searching for twin water cisterns. There are a lot more of those around here than silos. If they find anything, he'll contact you, Brandie."

"Our primary objective is to find Toby," Mitch said.

Brandie's pocket vibrated and tweeted indicating she had a text message. Everyone held their breath while she slid her finger across the screen. "It's my mom. Excuse me a second." She went into the storage room and called as her mom had asked.

"I know you said you'd call when you had more information, but Sadie asked me to pass along a message."

Her heart stopped. She couldn't feel it beating in her chest. If the woman had called her mother, then she hadn't wanted the people in that room to know.

"What…what did she say?"

"She just wants you to call her when you have a moment alone, but she left a new number."

"Would you text it to me, Mom?" She was glad her mother didn't know about Sadie's betrayal yet. It was the only way they'd both stayed calm.

"Sure. Are you all right, honey? Want me to come to the café? I could fix lunch for everyone."

"No, ma'am. They're about to leave. I'll be…I'm going to…to, um, the courthouse. They think I'll be safe while they follow up on some leads." She fibbed to ease her mother's mind.

"That's good. You shouldn't be alone. I'll text this to you. Just let me know if you need me. I love you."

"Bye. Love you, too."

Brandie did feel alone. As much as she didn't want to make decisions, that's exactly what she had to do. Tell Mitch? Not tell Mitch? She couldn't risk it. After they all left, she'd call Sadie and do whatever that horrible witch said to do if it would get her son back.

"You okay?" Mitch asked. "I was just locking up when Beth said you guys were staying."

"That's right."

"I'd feel more comfortable if I hung around, too, then."

"Honestly, you're taking being in charge of me way too seriously." She had to get rid of him. He'd never leave her alone long enough to make the call or allow her to meet Sadie. "Don't worry about me and just go do your job. You are still a Texas Ranger, right? It certainly doesn't seem like you quit. You probably lied about that so you could keep tabs on me."

"Brandie, what's going on? Who were you talking to?"

"My mother. See? You are not responsible for me. I take it back. I hate other people always making decisions for me. Hate it." She raised her voice and shoved past him back into the dining area.

"Not a problem. But I'm not falling for it. It's too convenient. Let me see your phone."

"We're friends, Mitch. You really don't get it, do you?"

"I don't believe that you got a phone call and suddenly you can't stand me."

"So now I'm a liar and don't know my own feelings?" She had to hold it together. "See for yourself. It was my mom. No one ordered me to do anything. I just came to my senses. I don't like all the looks and everyone assuming we're a couple."

Mitch checked out her call history. Deep confusion was in his eyes when he locked eyes with her and returned her phone. "I'm sorry. I…"

"Should have believed me?" She slipped her finger over the volume button and turned the phone to silent so when the text from her mom came through, no one would know. "I get enough of that at home."

The horrible implied meaning, accusing him of being like her father, was loud and clear to him. He stood straighter. Stiff. Lips flattened just like when he'd first worked for her and watched everything from a distance.

Would he forgive her? If she came home with Toby, maybe he would. If she helped Sadie with drugs or guns… would he forgive her then? It went against everything he'd been working for his entire adult life. But she didn't have a choice. She had to choose Toby even if she loved Mitch.

She drew in a sharp breath at the realization of just how much she loved them both. They'd slowly become a family over the past six months. Mitch was everything she wanted. Nothing like her father as she'd implied. He'd proven that to her, even while doing his job as a Ranger.

"I'm sorry, too. If I had cooperated yesterday we could have prevented most of this misunderstanding. You would have figured out it was Sadie before she came here today." *Remain strong. Don't let him see how sorry you really are.*

She followed him through the door, standing in front of the café. The thing that had been all-consuming until a few days ago. She could lose the family business, but she couldn't lose her family.

"It was Andrea who put everything together, not me. Those women wouldn't have been here to talk if you hadn't kicked us out. I guess everything happened just like it was supposed to." Mitch had a sad look in his eyes. "I know things aren't right between us."

"I think Cord's waiting on you."

"I just want to say that you're, uh… You really are the strongest and bravest person I've met. You'll get through this just fine and so will Toby. We'll find him and I'll be out of your hair for good."

He gently tugged her hand from massaging her neck. He kissed it, squeezed it and walked away.

"What's that all about? Isn't she coming?" Cord asked in the truck.

"Drive around the block and let me out back." Mitch could tell when Brandie was lying. Her mom had called, but something was wrong. Brandie had changed after that.

"You going to tell me why?"

"You need to check on the Quinns or send a deputy. Someone might be in Brandie's house, using their phones."

"You think Sadie was in touch with Brandie? I think she articulated exactly why she didn't want you around."

"Articulate all you want. I've been around Brandie a lot

of hours in the past six months. She's lying. I just don't know why." Mitch felt her lack of trust like a knife twisting from his belly to his backbone.

"I told you not to get too involved. It always complicates things."

"You told me not to get involved with a suspect. Brandie's not a suspect."

"And that's part of your problem, Mitch. You weren't and still aren't looking at the facts." Cord stopped the truck on the back side of the garage. "Brandie's given us plenty of reasons not to trust her, to doubt her story. We still don't know how or why King was able to blackmail her."

"It was a legit reason to her."

"She told you." He put the truck in Park, throwing an arm across the top of the seat. "But you aren't going to tell me. Dammit, Lieutenant. I imagine ordering you to disclose the information won't do me a hell of a lot of good? At least tell me if it's relative to any possible shipment that's—"

"No, sir. It's a private matter."

"You're going to follow her?"

"I'm burnin' daylight, sir."

"Get out of my truck." Cord lowered the window as Mitch shut the door. "Pete's got a deputy posted to make sure she stays put. And Beth's inside. Oh, and Mitch? I hope she is lying. You two are good together."

Chapter Twenty-Two

Mitch planned to follow Brandie when she left the garage. He assumed she'd get a phone call blackmailing her to do something questionable. Every part of his investigative ability told him that. His stubborn boss was bound to get herself into a boatload of trouble attempting to get her son back on her own.

It wouldn't take long. Sadie—or whatever her name was—had gotten to her. He didn't blame Brandie for any of it. He'd do anything for Toby, too. Anything.

Mitch heard car tires crunching the gravel lot and ducked to the edge of the building behind some used tires. If he followed in a car, particularly his car, Brandie would see it for miles. That left him with one choice. He had to get inside Brandie's car, which was still parked in the garage.

Luck was on his side that their argument had interrupted him setting the building alarm. He still had his keys. He snuck inside and then was at a loss how to hide his six-two body in the backseat of a compact car. Unless...

Faster than he thought possible, he popped the hood, disconnected two essential wires and dropped his keys on the desk before running outside again. If Brandie was in a hurry, she wouldn't think twice about borrowing his car. He unlocked the door with the spare he had tied under the frame.

The sleeping bag and stuff they'd taken with them to King's massacre was still in his car and easy to toss over him. He pulled off his jacket, balled it under his head and got as comfortable as he could on the floorboard.

It had only been a few minutes when something tapped the side of the car and he heard keys jingling. The engine purred as she gunned it a couple of times. Beth's voice was outside along with a banging against the windows. "At least let me go with you!" she shouted as Brandie sharply turned right.

Mitch should have removed the gun Cord had loaned him from the small of his back. Every bump the car hit jarred a part of it into his flesh. She moved the seat closer to the wheel, which gave him a little relief. He looked at his watch—five minutes and he should reveal that he was there.

Wait. He needed to know that her phone call wasn't with the kidnappers. His phone was already on silent. He slipped it into his palm, swiped open the camera, hit Record and squeezed it between the seat and the door.

It took two tries, but he hadn't seen her phone. She was completely absorbed in driving the car and looking in the mirror.

"Deputy Hardy, you need to go back to town. We just crossed the county line and okay, that's it. Yep. Head on home now."

Mitch hoped she was talking to herself.

The car sped up and then slammed to a halt. The gun pinched, his legs cramped, his head shook but he kept his mouth shut and his body covered in case she was looking over the seat. He'd never thought of his car as small before. Now he did.

"You can sit up now. Nobody's around."

He sat on the seat, stretching his legs in blessed relief. "When did you know?"

"My car was perfectly fine yesterday. And you would never have left your car keys on the desk." She glared at him in the mirror. "How did you know I was lying?"

"You have a couple of tells. Grabbing your neck for one. That's something you do when you're exhausted, though. The real tell is when you twist your mouth a lot."

"Okay, thanks. I needed to know when I meet the chess Queen. Now get out."

"No way."

"Seriously, Mitch. I can't bring anyone with me. She'll know."

"As far as she knows I'm just a mechanic. I'm not letting you go on your own." Nope. He was with her for the duration. Period.

"She was listening to everything in the café."

Mitch shook his head and leaned through the armrest between the front seats. "Not a chance. She's lying. If they had been, she would have known about the drugs and that we didn't have them. That's just my educated opinion, of course."

"You know, I never asked for your opinion. I was quite happy in my life before all this started in my garage. Totally ignorant of drug smugglers and undercover agents."

"Not leaving the car." He stared at her with his head cocked sideways. She could have injured him pretty badly if she'd used her elbow to hit his face. But she wasn't that kind of woman. She didn't react that way. Oh, wait, she had knocked him out with a lamp.

Either way, it made him more determined to stay. She needed him. He could react quicker and before the thought crossed her mind that she was in danger.

"Even if she explicitly said not to bring anyone?"

He was staying. "What are we supposed to do?"

"I have to call her and let her know I lost whoever they had following me." Her hands flexed around the steering wheel. "I just want it all to end. Can we do that? Can we get my son back and get back to normal?"

"Yes." A pitiful remark bounced into his head. Something about how he was a little hurt that she hadn't trusted him. The serious part of himself that he'd discovered since Cord had used the words *daddy crush* held him back. This wasn't about him. They would get back to normal. That's who they were.

"Then let's call the witch and get on with it," she said.

Before she had her cell in her hand, Mitch's pocket was vibrating. "It's Pete."

"Put it on speaker or you're out of the car."

"Yeah?" he said, holding the cell over the seat back.

"Great, you answered. Put me on speaker if you're still with Brandie," Pete said.

"You already are. What do you need?"

"We have an Alpine address for a Patrice Orlando and we're ninety percent certain it's the blonde we're looking for. Her background and timeline fit. She travels across the border a lot. I've got an Alpine unit heading there now."

"She won't be at her place. She told Brandie to lose the tail and call, indicating she's sending her somewhere else. We're just about to do that. I'll mute my phone so you can listen in."

Brandie dialed.

"It took you long enough. If you want your precious little Toby back with all his fingers and toes, then you'll do exactly what I say. I need you to go to the border station in Presidio. When you arrive, you'll verify that the four women who have listed you as their employer are telling the truth. Give them a ride to the post office."

"Will Toby be waiting for me there?"

"Honey." She stopped to laugh. "Toby's safe for the moment. He thinks he's at summer camp. You get those women to my contact and we'll talk again."

Sadie, also known now as Patrice, disconnected, sounding confident that Brandie would follow through with whatever was commanded.

"Those women are smuggling drugs, aren't they?"

"Most likely." He adjusted the phone between them. "Did you catch all that, Beth?"

"Yes. Brandie, do exactly what she says. I've got this end covered. There will be DEA agents there to follow those women. You won't be breaking the law, you'll be helping us."

"She'll probably have someone watching me once I get to Presidio. I should drop Mitch—"

"I'm staying."

"That's ridiculous. Are the women going to sit on top of you?"

"We'll have the building covered," Beth said. "Brandie, drop him off a couple of blocks from the post office."

"Mind if I ride up front?"

"Sure. I even promise not to leave you on the side of the road."

He was in and out of the car faster than a speeding bullet. "This is weird for me, you know."

"What?"

"I've never ridden in this seat before or in the backseat for that matter."

"Well, you can't drive to—"

"It's fine. Just…different." Mitch stretched out.

"You should put your seat belt on. You can never tell if aliens will be landing on the highway. Or a deer. Be safe."

"So, do a lot of aliens land in broad daylight?" He buckled up whether he thought he needed to or not. It made her happy. And he liked cheering her up a bit.

"Well, they are more likely to land at night, I'll give you that. Do you have any sunglasses?"

"No, but I do have some very expensive shades." He took the case from the glove compartment, wiped the lenses with the cloth he kept them wrapped inside and handed them to her.

"Nice. They really cut the glare. Why don't you wear these all the time? Instead of the ten-dollar pair you usually have."

"We're closing in on Patrice Orlando because of her shoes. I didn't think that a two-hundred-dollar pair of shades fit my nomad mechanic background."

"Smart, but I might just steal these."

"I'll buy you your own pair." He could. He'd been collecting a paycheck for almost three years with no expenses.

She swished her head quickly to the side and the glasses slid down her nose. Instead of the cute O-shaped lips he thought he'd see, she scrunched up her nose to stop their descent.

"You will not spend that kind of money on me for a pair of sunglasses."

"But you like them."

She shook her head and her free hand shot up behind her neck. "Stop kidding around and tell me what I need to know when we get to Presidio. You have about forty minutes to turn me into a secret agent."

He stared at her, surprised by how her words affected him. She'd probably meant it to be funny. But he was suddenly frightened like he'd never been before. He'd had years of driving highways by himself, pulling over drunks or drug dealers. He'd been cautious but not frightened.

The thought that Brandie would be in the middle of everything. That she'd run into any type of fight to protect Toby at any cost... The thought of losing either one of them chilled him to his marrow.

Chapter Twenty-Three

Mitch had talked for the entire drive, and Brandie had listened. He explained that he knew Presidio, having been on assignment there last fall. They'd taken side street after side street until he'd pointed her back in the right direction. With one turn she'd have a straight shot back to the main road. He was about to be on foot four blocks away from the post office, but said he'd be there in plenty of time to make sure her drop-off went smoothly.

"If you act too calm, then whoever's watching you is going to get suspicious," Mitch told her with his hand on the handle ready to jump from the car. "Remember, there's a company of Texas Rangers looking for Toby. Along with troopers, deputies and everyone else they can snag. You do your part here and we've got your back."

"Andrea is really imposing on her father?" Brandie shook her head, still unable to process what they were all doing for her. "I can't believe she asked Homeland Security to track down Sadie's—I mean, Patrice Orlando's possible family or other real estate. I know everything's being done that can be done."

"I know you probably meant what you said in the café. I'm not trying to be a dictator. What I'm trying to do—"

"Is save my life and get Toby back." She covered his

cheek with her hand, and he leaned into her palm, kissing it. "I'm sorry, I didn't really mean it."

There had been very few kisses between them. How could she know that this man was hers? It probably didn't make sense to the normal couple. But they were like two attracting magnets, unable to stay apart. When he was around, she forced herself to stay away from him. She'd said that she wanted their lives back to normal, but that was far from the truth.

Things had to be different. No more boss lady and mechanic. She wanted him as a boyfriend in every way possible. Even on the way to vouch for illegal alien drug smugglers.

"Will ya kiss me so we can get this part over and done?" She smiled hesitantly, wondering how he'd react or if the request was completely out of line. Then he pulled her to meet him halfway.

His lips slashed across hers—full of tension, control and desire. His tongue slid into her mouth completely at home. It didn't seem like their third or fourth kiss. It seemed like something they'd been sharing every early morning and every late night. Both of them were reluctantly pulling away, putting an end to a very precious moment.

"For the record, *that part* will never be over and done with."

He ducked out of the car and was gone before she had both hands back on the wheel. She pressed the gas and would be at the border station in a matter of minutes. Kissing might not have been the appropriate thing, but it had bolstered her resolve. Had some of his courage shot into her?

Mitch had told her twice how brave he thought she was, how strong. Yet, she was always so frightened. She'd always been frightened of losing everything. Since her mechanic had come to work, she'd grown into that strong woman he saw and encouraged her to be. She parked the car and made it inside because of Mitch's faith.

Her hands shook when she handed her driver's license to be copied and completed the paperwork. The women looked like ordinary teenagers. Brandie assumed they'd been thoroughly searched and must have swallowed the drugs. At least none of them looked ill. They actually didn't look scared or concerned about any part of the process.

They were out the door, one calling "shotgun" as they took off running in their pretty heels and short skirts. The tight-fitting T-shirts showed off slim, young figures. They chattered away in Spanish, not caring who she was or why she was there.

It took only a few minutes to get to the post office. She looked around for a car or someone who was Sadie's contact. But as soon as she parked in a spot, the girls were out the door and waving as they walked in four different directions.

Following them wasn't her responsibility. Toby was. She didn't see anyone moving after the women, but what was she supposed to? If they were covertly there she couldn't tell. She didn't see Mitch, either.

She tapped the leather steering wheel cover with a broken nail. If she'd been in her car, a file would be in the change holder. Waiting on the phone call, she tried to even the ragged edge. She needed someone to tell her what to do past this point. She'd kept her end of the bargain—twice. She'd broken the law—twice. Where was her son?

There wasn't a soul in sight. The street had been empty since the four women had gone their separate ways. She hadn't asked specifically about her next step. Maybe they'd meant to go inside the post office. She cracked the door open and her cell rang, making her jump out of her skin.

"Be at the border station same time tomorrow."

"Sadie, please. Please tell me where Toby is. He must be scared. I promise to do anything you need me to do. I'm begging you to give him back."

"You have too many law enforcement friends, Brandie. I'll call tomorrow with an address. For now…he's safe and one more night away from you is just an adventure." She disconnected.

"No!" Brandie threw her cell into the opposite floorboard. "No!" she screamed, hitting the dash with both of her fists. "No, no, no!" She grabbed the wheel and shaking the car. She rested her head on the horn and cried.

She could have sworn that there weren't any tears left, but she'd been wrong. She had to meet Mitch. They had a pre-arranged meeting, and he'd probably been waiting for her a good ten minutes.

The engine of his car reminded her of him. Fine-tuned, quiet and when you stepped on the gas it raced ninety to nothing. He leaned against the wall of the building, head down with a splash of graffiti at his back. She barely braked for a stop before he opened the door and slid down in the seat so he couldn't be seen.

He pushed her phone away from his feet with his boot. "Did she call with a location?"

"No." The single word choked her up, but she kept driving. They were out of Presidio and heading back to Marfa.

"Brandie, pull over. Come on, sweetie, let's slow down."

She glanced at the speedometer. They were going eighty-five. She eased off the gas and slowed, turning to stop on an old overgrown road.

"Sorry."

"I think it's better if I drive us back and you tell me what happened. Let's meet at the hood."

They got out, but all she could think about was wringing that thirty-something-year-old neck. She threw her fisted hands in the air, screaming her frustrations to the late-afternoon sun. A picture-perfect blue-sky day. Ironically, she'd be picking her son up from day care about now.

It was the slowest time at the café so she spent it with Toby.

Mitch handed her a rock as big as her hand. He spun her to face the field. "Throw it."

"What?"

"Just do it."

When she'd let it go like a wimp, he opened her palm and set another giant rock on it. Then another, repeating the process until she was exhausted and tears ran down her face.

Mitch spun her again, but this time he held on to her. She buried her face against the soft comforting cotton of his T-shirt.

"She said nothing. If I want my son back I have to show up here tomorrow. Do the same thing. What if she says to come back again? How many days do I do this? How many times before Toby gives up that I'm coming to get him?"

His strong arms wrapped her tight. The safer she felt, the worse she felt that Toby wasn't there, too.

"I can't tell you that Toby isn't scared or missing you. You'd never believe me anyway." He spoke above her head. The sun blazed its descent in the sky. "But you know that he loves you. He'll heal. We'll make sure of that."

The sound of a telephone ringing was faint in the background. It took a second for her to realize her cell was in the car. Mitch's cell buzzed in his denim jacket.

"Yeah? Wait and slow down a second. Putting you all on speaker." They ran back to the car so they could hear the conference call.

THEY NEEDED A BREAK in this case. Toby had been missing long enough. No matter how strong Brandie acted, it was still an act. He'd hate to see her shut down like she talked about that morning. He couldn't bear that.

Everyone was finally connected to the call, lots of voices talking to others around them. Mitch and Brandie were silent. Waiting. He tried to be patient and was about to take the phone when she frustratingly spoke up.

"Excuse me. What's going on?"

The voices quieted.

"We've found her. Believe it or not her real name is Patty Johnson aka Patrice Orlando, aka Sadie Dillon. She owns a lot of property. One is a newer place where her mother lives in Presidio, 642 Bledsoe Boulevard," Andrea said.

"Do you really think Toby's there?" Brandie asked from the passenger seat, holding the cell between them. "Does anyone know if that's where my son is being held?"

"We're less than ten minutes out." Mitch put the car in gear, the tires spun dirt and dust into the still air. "We'll look. It's worth a try. Sadie, Patrice or Patty—whatever her name is—she doesn't know we're onto her or she would have upped the stakes for Toby's return. She thinks she has all the time in the world. That's why she thinks she can order you back here tomorrow."

"She did what?" Andrea asked.

"We're sending county backup." Pete's connection wasn't as strong, but they still heard him give commands. "You can't go in until I get a team there. If I call Presidio

PD they'll go in hot and we'll lose the advantage. We don't want that. You got it?"

"I'm obtaining a search warrant," Cord told them. "We need to be sure about this. Once we go in, our target is going to know everything."

"Okay, we'll watch the place to see if there are any signs of Toby," Mitch told them, knowing in his gut that he wouldn't wait if they saw him. Screw the case. He and Brandie weren't taking any chances with a delayed rescue.

"Mitch, I'm repeating myself," Pete said clearly. "I want you to hear me. Do. Not. Approach. That. House."

"I hear you, Sheriff." They'd do what was needed.

"But—"

"Hang up." He cut Brandie off before she could ask about any exceptions. It was better to ask forgiveness than break a direct order. He knew that it didn't matter. Pete knew he was lying through his teeth. The man had gone against Homeland Security to protect the woman he loved.

"You can wait if you want to. I'm getting Toby." Brandie tossed his cell on the dashboard and crossed her arms.

"I know."

She wouldn't be silent for long. There weren't many streets in Presidio. He knew where to head and even knew what side of Main Street the house number indicated. He didn't know what they were heading to, but one thing was certain. He'd protect them both. They needed a fast, safe way to do it.

"A simple way to check out the house and not alert them is to get invited inside."

"How do you suppose we do that? And don't you think they know who we are? She worked at the café for over two months."

"We can hope that whoever is inside doesn't know what you or I look like." He wasn't crazy about this next part, but waiting for Pete's men and the warrant would be harder. "I can raise the hood, act like we're having car problems. Do you think you can go to the door and ask for water? I can hang back, cover you and cross my fingers they ask us both."

"Can we go in without a warrant? I thought that was illegal."

"Not if whoever's in that house invites us. We'll take a look around, see if we need to tip our hand to our opponent. I'd hate to lose that advantage if we don't have to. If we get inside and Toby's there, we don't need a warrant, either." He coaxed her hand into his, getting her to really look at him.

"What if Sadie is inside?"

He shrugged because she knew the answer. "We can wait around the corner for Pete's men. It's your call."

"You know I'll do anything for my son."

"So will I."

Chapter Twenty-Four

"Iron gates, three sides iron fence, brick wall on the east with a twenty-foot easement. The windows give them a pretty good view of anything on the street."

Brandie heard cussing as Mitch gave the report. He'd left the speaker on without Brandie asking this time. When circling the block, they'd made notes from a distance and parked on the far north side of the house. They'd talked themselves out of approaching the house.

"No way to observe who's inside. Garage is closed. Can't tell what type of vehicles it's holding. Curtains closed, dark. There are lights on. I'm not close enough to determine shadows if anyone passes."

"What you're telling me is that they've got a 360 degree view. There's no possible way we'll get surveillance on the inside to see if Toby's there."

"It gets worse. There's a field at the back of the house."

This time Brandie wanted to join in on the cussing.

"Then that means we serve the warrant. ETA for my deputies is nineteen minutes. We're right behind them. They'll be there by the time we determine what to do," Pete said in the background. Cord was in the same vehicle heading to Presidio. "Don't do anything stupid."

They disconnected, and Mitch looked through his binoculars again.

"I don't know where either of those men get off telling us not to do anything stupid. They've both put their lives at risk more than once for the ones they loved." Brandie refused to cry and lose her determination. "Isn't it my decision? Don't I have any say in what happens?"

Mitch set the binoculars in his lap. "They're being overly cautious."

"They want to do everything by the rules and they're forgetting that the most precious thing to me in the world may be in that house."

"Dammit. There's a car pulling out of the driveway. I can't see the tag number, but it looks like the make and model of the blonde Queen's."

The woman had so many names, they'd given up on using any at all. It was ironic because Brandie felt like she'd been doing nothing except bowing to the woman's will for the past two days.

"I'm not waiting." She reached over and turned the key. "Let's go."

And just like that they were on their way. It was a knee-jerk reaction needing to do something herself to get Toby back in her arms. Mitch stopped at the first corner, a worried look clouding his eyes.

"Remember, you'll have to leave your cell phone in the car. Think of a reason why neither one of us would have one or they couldn't be used. Be mad at me—it'll cover the nervousness."

She nodded. They'd been over this several times, but as soon as he'd mentioned nerves, she'd realized how horribly nervous she was. "What do I need to look for? Besides the obvious, that is."

Her hands were shaking even with her fingers laced together.

"Listen for other people. Someone trying to keep Toby

quiet. See if you can get into the kitchen. Look for kid food. Ask for a map or to use the phone. You're a smart woman, Brandie. You got this."

"You're sure this is the right thing?"

"No. I'm not. I'm impatient to get this over with, too. Look, if you have any doubts…it's fifteen minutes. Just fifteen minutes." He shook his head and reached for the key. "I shouldn't have suggested you do this. It's too dangerous. We'll wait."

"What if she's leaving with him right now, taking Toby to another location that isn't one of her properties? If no one follows her we might lose him forever. I'll stay here and watch the house. You go after the car." She opened the door. He caught the back of her jacket as she swung her legs outside.

"I'm not going to let you do something so —"

"Stupid?" She relaxed her arms and came free of the jacket as she got out and slammed the door. "You don't control my actions, Mitch Striker."

She pointed in the direction the car had left, hoping and praying that he wouldn't jump out and throw her back inside. She was no match for his strength or up to another debate on what was the right or wrong move. She turned and ran down the edge of the street. She'd watch the house from behind the brick wall. It was beginning to get dark and there were no streetlights to expose her.

Mitch's car engine seemed loud, but no one inside would pay any attention to it. He drove straight, and she headed back to the house. It was a relief not to argue with him. Making a decision and moving forward was scary but she'd done it.

Brandie hadn't realized that the wall was just a little shorter than her. She had to stand on tiptoes to peek over it. She walked even with the backyard, searching it again for signs that a little boy had been playing there.

Nothing. And no movement in the house. She ran back to the opposite end of the wall straight into a very large man with a very large shotgun pointed at her. He jerked the barrel toward the house. So much for her secret agent training.

The man shoved her inside the garage door. "Sit. Cross your legs. Keep your hands behind your head."

She complied since she didn't really have a choice. He had a gun and she had nothing. He slid his hands across her sides as she sat, removing her cell and smashing it under his boot.

The two-car garage looked new with neatly stacked boxes on metal shelves against the back wall. It was unusual that there were two windows, both barricaded with bars. No tools, either, for yard work or for a car. And no escape as he pushed a button, shutting the door and closing it at her back.

He stood silently in the corner, gun pointed at her casually. She wasn't a threat. They both knew it, just like they both knew she couldn't talk her way out. Her legs were beginning to cramp when the door leading to the house opened.

"Sadie, where's Toby?"

"Well, hello to you, too." Her son's kidnapper acted like they were long-lost friends. She was still in her chic outfit, beautiful studded shoes clicking against the concrete floor. "This could have been so easy. You do as I say and Toby would have mysteriously turned up tomorrow. You could have created any story and everyone would have believed it."

She was wrong, but Brandie wasn't going to argue.

"I go by Patrice, and if you found this place, then you already know that."

Her palm stung Brandie's cheek without warning.

"You have complicated my life beyond your small comprehension level.

"*Mamacita*, pack only what you need. ¡*Vámonos*!" she called through the door then took the shotgun away from the man standing guard. "Go help her. Only essentials. Remind her of our talk."

The man stepped inside.

"I don't have time for you." She rested the shotgun against the wall near the door button, replacing it with a handgun she pulled from one of the open boxes.

"Just give me Toby and we'll sit here out of your way long after you're gone."

She flipped open another box and began loading the pistol. "I'm afraid we both know that won't work. If you're here, I can assume that Mitch is chasing after our decoy. Was he hiding in the trunk when you picked up the girls? I should have known that he wouldn't keep his nose out of your business. He's clearly got a thing for you since he wouldn't look twice at me." She spun around, gun at her waist. Her long blond hair was free, straight and past her shoulders.

Although she was very beautiful, her face was full of hatred. Gone was the woman who happily waited on tables, smacked gum and brought Toby Mexican jumping beans. The evil seemed to ooze from every motion, but especially her eyes. Brandie knew what the gun was for. Her.

"You can use us as hostages. I'll cooperate. I swear. Just don't hurt Toby."

"Don't be ridiculous. *Mamacita* would kill me if I hurt your little boy. She's taken quite a shine to him. We can raise him to use his pale skin to our advantage. Don't doubt that. But you, on the other hand. You are just a sacrificial pawn. I might let you say goodbye to your son if you tell me what they know."

"I have no idea. It's just me and Mitch, exactly like you said. He came to help me. We saw your car leave so we split up."

"Don't lie to me!" she screamed. "I had everything planned to perfection, every move carefully calculated. Then you came into the picture and hired a mechanic who would never leave. Rey screwed everything up by kidnapping your kid."

"That wasn't a part of the plan?" Brandie asked, genuinely surprised that her son was an afterthought, but had brought down this woman who thought of herself as the queen of an organization.

"Of course not! Too many variables." She paced back and forth. One, two, three steps, then back. Mumbling to herself. "Magnus Carlsen. Think like Carlsen. His end game."

Brandie was at a loss, not comprehending the conversation, witnessing the demise of a desperate woman. She paced erratically, mumbled and tapped her temple with the weapon.

She finally looked up, pointing the gun at Brandie like an extension of her finger. "That's what I need. One of Carlsen's famous endgames. I have the strongest pieces. I should move them into position and be able to take out no matter what opponent shows its face. Like your knight mechanic."

Sadie still didn't know that Mitch was an undercover Ranger. That fact had to be in their favor. Her knight? Images of a giant game board with life-size playing pieces sped through her mind. Rey sat as the king. Sadie next to him. But in what game would the queen take down her own? That was just it. Sadie was the dark queen and the rest of them were playing opposite her.

"This isn't a game," she said, trying to bring Sadie back to reality.

"Of course it is. I make a move and someone counters. You're simply a passed pawn, something to exchange for what I want."

"If you exchange someone, exchange Toby. He—"

"Shut up and let me think."

Mitch had to be outside by now along with Pete, Cord and the rest of Presidio County's sheriff's department. If she knew for certain, she could run to the button on the wall and open the garage door. She uncrossed her legs, getting life back into them before making a mad dash. She gained only a momentary glare from her captor who still paced.

Trying to reach the opener was useless until she knew someone was outside. She hadn't heard anything. Nothing from inside the house. No cars leaving. How was everyone escaping?

"Can I please see my son? You said he was inside, right?"

Sadie stopped in her tracks, eyes clear and evil. "Do you think I'm stupid?" She pointed the gun, it didn't waver like when she was thinking. "You're staying exactly where you are."

Brandie really wished that Mitch had given her some physical secret agent training. She desperately wanted to know how to leap forward, take the gun from Sadie and find Toby.

The doorbell rang. And rang again. The doorbell did multiple rings until Sadie/Patrice/Patty Johnson lost her temper at the annoyance. She threw her head forward, flipping her hair with an irritated growl.

This was Brandie's chance. She pushed up from the floor as quickly as she could and threw herself at Sadie as she lifted her head. They toppled backward, tumbling into the metal shelves, knocking the boxes to the concrete.

Guns and boxes of ammo fell in every direction. They continued to spin across the smooth surface while Sadie yanked, tugged and jerked on all of Brandie's clothes, trying to stop her from getting to the garage opener button on the wall.

Brandie's boots slipped on the slick surface, and she fell to her knees. Sadie was on top of her. They rolled. Sadie pulled hair and clawed. All Brandie could do was protect herself.

Then Brandie's head cracked to the right, reacting to the butt of the gun hitting her jaw. She saw shards of light and felt the world sort of phasing out.

Toby!

She couldn't let this witch take her little boy. If she wanted a fight…she'd get a fight. Brandie fought the haze gathering in her head, pushing, punching the blonde madwoman in her scrawny sides.

Kicking out from under her, Brandie rolled, then crawled until she could get her feet under her. Sadie had hold of her boot when there was a loud crash. They froze.

Brandie turned and scooted away, but Sadie didn't care. She was on her feet and running inside. Brandie should wait on Mitch. She knew that. The lack of sounds within the house earlier frightened her. There had been others in the house. She'd heard them moving, talking. Then she hadn't.

If she wanted Toby…she should go after wherever that crazy woman had taken him.

Chapter Twenty-Five

The deputies couldn't just shatter the front door with a ram. They had to pry the iron bars off the front, then crash through. The car he'd followed was a decoy. Some sixteen-year-old kid had been hired to drive it to the border. As soon as Mitch had gotten a look and verified the car was empty, he'd headed back to the house.

There was a chance that during that time, Brandie had been found and everyone inside had driven away. He swallowed hard, controlling his emotions as Cord crushed his ribs holding him back from entering the house first.

The sheriff's department searched. No shots were fired. Pete walked out the door, shaking his head, and Mitch was finally released. He ran, jumped the short iron fence, ignoring the gate.

"Are they in there? Are they...?" Mitch doubled over. His head dropped below his belt before he fell to his knees. "This is my fault. I shouldn't have left her alone. I shouldn't have waited on warrants and procedure."

The pain shooting through his heart was unbearable. He didn't want to live without Brandie and Toby. They'd become his life, the most important things to him. He couldn't imagine losing them to a waitress he'd always call Sadie Dillon. It was so bizarre, he couldn't wrap his head around their deaths.

"Mitch, they aren't inside, man. No one is," Pete said, grabbing Mitch's shoulder to get him to stand.

"Then there's a chance. What do you want me to do?"

"I've got my men canvassing the neighbors. I doubt they'll give us any workable information. We'll set up to watch her other properties, but I think she's smarter than that."

"Until she resurfaces or makes demands," Cord said.

"You want me to sit and wait? That's why we're in this mess." That was the last thing he'd do. "I waited on the right way to do things. I waited and gave her time to make her chesslike moves. I can't do that now. I need to find my family."

The men looked at each other. Neither seemed surprised.

"I'm going inside." He stuck his hand out to Cord. "Give me my sidearm."

Cord complied and stayed in the dry, lifeless yard. Mitch shoved past a deputy who said "hey" and attempted to stop him while Pete shouted the okay.

Mitch didn't care about anyone else. They could all assume they'd all cleared out. But he'd been on the major road in town. He hadn't seen many cars. He'd looked at every face. And his gut told him to keep trying. He'd keep searching until he found them. Period.

Men were in different rooms looking for anything the warrant allowed. Someone was coming down from the attic. "Nothing there."

Mitch secured his weapon at the small of his back when he realized none of these men knew he was a Ranger. He straddled a dining-room chair. How could they have gotten out of this house? It looked every bit like a normal house. But it wasn't. It belonged to a smuggler.

What did smugglers have?

"Tap on the walls and move furniture. There may be a hidey-hole." He yelled loud, told some twice as he pulled the china cabinet to look behind it.

Nothing. He searched every inside wall and started for the garage. There had to be something.

"Striker!" Deputy Hardy called. "I found something. I looked inside after I saw the laundry basket in the bathtub. I mean you wouldn't do that, right? Laundry goes to the— Anyway, it looks like it goes under the house."

At the bottom of a bathroom linen closet was a panel with a small finger hole. It looked like extra access to the water pipes and it might be. Except this was wide enough for a man twice his size to fit through. He pulled his weapon and reached to lift the wood.

Hardy jerked his arm back stopping him. "I understand why you have that weapon, but I'm going to have to ask you to hand it over to me, sir."

"I'm afraid I can't do that."

Hardy drew his sidearm. "Damn it, Mitch. I can take care of this. Hand me your gun."

The youngest deputy in the sheriff's department was shifting nervously. Mitch hated what he was about to do, but he couldn't tell him he was undercover. Hell, he might not be. He had resigned and not proceeded back to Austin like his orders had stated.

He wasn't taking a chance. He was heading down that hidey-hole.

Hardy readjusted his grip to reach for his radio. Mitch slammed his forearm up under Hardy's gun, knocking it to the floor. He ripped the radio from the stunned deputy's belt and shoved him backward through the door. Locking it while Hardy recovered and began shouting and turning the knob.

"Run, tell Pete," he mumbled. "I'm going to need backup."

Mitch quickly pulled the hole cover only to find it spring back into place. He lifted again, wishing he'd grabbed Hardy's flashlight. He unlocked and cracked the door open. No reason to delay the cavalry. He propped the panel open with a stick located on the underside, secured both weapons, then lowered himself through the hole.

As soon as his feet hit concrete, his gun was back in his hand. He took a second to let his eyes adjust. But immediately he could see light at the end of a long tunnel. Then he heard voices. Arguing.

His heart raced as fast as his feet wanted to move, but he held himself in check. His fingers felt a rough, concrete block wall behind him. This place had been specifically built for smuggling.

The tunnel led to the back of the house. Judging from the voices and the far sliver of light, it probably led the full distance of the field behind the house, too. Three feet wide and at least fifty yards long. There was no way to find the exit without walking through this end. He had a few minutes before the sheriff could follow.

He hugged the wall, staying flush to it as best he could.

"Shoot her and be done with it. We've taken much too much time here," Sadie said, her distinctive voice shrill as it bounced through the tunnel.

"I thought I was a pawn to be traded for a better playing piece."

Brandie!

There were at least three people standing in the light. Sadie and whoever she'd been demanding shoot Brandie.

"We lift the door. She screams. We might as well put a bullet in our own heads."

The Spanish that followed was a deep bass and too fast

for Mitch to catch all of it. The pool of light grew larger until it was apparent there was another small area about ten feet wide like under the house. He could make out Sadie with one hand on a ladder rung. A figure was on the floor—Brandie. And a large outline with a hand extended as if to shoot.

The gun drooped back to his side. This time Mitch could understand the Spanish. "You shoot her then. I take care of your mother."

As the man handed Sadie the weapon, Mitch ran forward. "Drop the weapon."

"Mitch?"

Sadie did the opposite. She snatched the gun and fired. He dove, sliding across the pavement on the elbows of his jacket. The lightbulb shattered, spinning the room into darkness.

"Get next to the wall and don't move, Brandie," he called out as the large man kicked his thigh.

He heard a door or hatch open. Then a scream of frustration. By the sound of Sadie's curses, Brandie hadn't listened to him. She must have yanked Sadie's ankle and latched on in order to keep her from escaping.

The yelling continued while he stood. Fighting blind was nearly impossible. The man could be heading back down the tunnel for all he knew, but then a big fist connected with his kidney.

"Mitch, help! We can't let her go. Toby's already gone."

He headed toward the voice. She was right. They had to get Sadie off the ladder.

But a direct hit to his right kidney again made him spin and fire off a couple of punches—including one using the gun still in his fist. "You stop hitting me and you can take your chances out of this dark hole, man. All I want is your boss lady." He hoped he'd said the right words in Spanish.

"Mitch, I'm slipping."

"Okay," the big man answered.

Mitch pulled out his cell with his left hand and pressed on. It was a blinding light after so much complete darkness. He fixed everyone's positions in his head, stuck his phone back in his pocket and climbed the bottom two rungs to get Sadie. He wrapped his arm around her waist, and she immediately began clawing at his head.

Brandie fell to the floor as Mitch was rammed in his side. Obviously, the big man changed his mind about his freedom. Mitch didn't let go. He pulled his arms close against his ribs, taking another punch.

"Stay still, you rotten woman," Brandie said. Her hands tried to control the frantic flaying Sadie achieved while screaming at her man to kill them both.

He'd never hit a woman in his life and never intended to. Sadie was quickly changing his mind. He rolled several times, taking her with him in order to stop being her man's punching bag.

"Hang on to her, Mitch. Someone's coming," Brandie said from farther away, maybe down the tunnel.

"That should be the sheriff."

"Go! Kill the boy!" Sadie shouted.

"What?" Brandie cried. "You can't!"

Sadie was no longer as important as stopping the big man from leaving. Mitch shoved her off, got to his knees and leaped away from the lights coming through the tunnel. He grabbed the ladder rungs, just behind the big man making his escape.

"Send the men up after me, Brandie. I'm going to need their help." He didn't wait for an answer, but he heard another scuffle begin below and shouts of the deputies approaching.

The big man threw back the hatch, leaving a square

patch of dark bluish sky pinpricked with stars beginning their nightly West Texas reign. Mitch's ribs ached and his muscles tensed at the thought of seeing the big man's boot aiming for his head. He climbed, grabbed on to the top rung for his life and prepared his left forearm to block a kick.

Sure enough, the kick came. Mitch swung his arm around, locking his hand around the big man's ankle. With all his strength and a loud growl, he yanked, twisted and then pushed. His opponent tripped to the ground, and Mitch hurried out of the hole.

His opponent was lighter on his feet than he'd hoped. Mitch had both feet on the brittle grass and dirt just in time for another whack to the side of his head. He'd had enough and reached for his weapons...

"STOP! I SAID, STOP!" Sadie screamed with flashlights honing in on her face.

Their short scuffle for the loose gun had once again resulted with Brandie on the wrong end of the barrel. She was breathing hard, but at least on her feet.

"I swear I'll shoot her and you'll never find Toby."

The men behind the beams stopped. Sadie nervously shifted the gun between Brandie and the tunnel.

But most of the woman's focus was on the deputies. She didn't seem to notice Brandie inching a little closer along the wall when Sadie faced the tunnel. Brandie didn't know any defensive moves, but she put everything she had into a vicious kick against the back of Sadie's legs.

The blonde fell to her knees, the gun flew from her hand and landed across the tunnel. The men swooped in, pinning her to the ground while they cuffed her.

Pete pulled Brandie from the ladder, but she clung to it. Her son's life was at stake.

"Let me go! She told someone to shoot Toby. Mitch went after— You've got to help stop him."

Pete grabbed his radio from his belt. "We've got Brandie. Can you see the hatch exit?"

"Negative."

"Head north from the house. Mitch is there. I hear him fighting above me." Pete's eyebrows arched, asking an unspoken question.

Brandie let go of the rung and stepped to the side. "I'm fine. Please go help him."

Pete headed up the ladder.

"It doesn't matter," Sadie said with her face in the dirt. "You will not find that boy. He's gone. Without me you will *never* find him."

MITCH HEARD SADIE'S screeching words. His backup would be surfacing at any minute. He shrugged out of the denim jacket, needing the flexibility. He reached for one of the guns he'd had entering the tunnel but changed his mind. He couldn't shoot him or take a chance of accidentally wounding him in a fight over the weapon. The man he fought might have different ideas about negotiating a deal than his boss.

The man had at least fifty pounds on him. Mitch's strongest punches barely made him wince. He wove his fingers together and swung. The backhanded blow made the man stagger. Mitch threw one from the opposite direction. The man's head snapped to the side.

He fell backward like a tree toppling to the ground.

Pete's head popped out of the hatch. "Need some help?"

"Just cuff him." Mitch rested on his knees, catching his breath. His eyes were peeled on the road. "You have units headed here yet?"

"On their way. This thing—" he stomped on the hatch

"—is blocked from the street by that storage shed. Fairly smart on their part. Now where do you think they all headed?"

Pete slowly turned, searching the perimeter. He was too calm for Mitch's comfort. He joined him, nudging his shoulder when the unconscious man began to moan. The sheriff rolled the man to his stomach and added handcuffs to his wardrobe.

"Where the heck were these two planning on going?" Mitch asked, staring at the open lots.

"Do you think there's another tunnel?" Pete asked.

"Sir?" the radio blared into the quiet night.

"Go ahead."

"Brandie's demanding to come up the ladder now. That okay with you?"

"I'd prefer that she return to the secured house, but I take it that's not an option?" Pete looked at the hatch and leaned down to help Brandie up.

Mitch walked toward the road. Toby was still out there. They'd missed him by minutes and needed to find him. Not later. Right now. Nothing against Pete, but they didn't know what they were facing.

The entire neighborhood had to be watching. They all had to be aware of what was going on. Somebody had to have seen something. The people in the house had to have gone somewhere.

"Vehicles," he mumbled. "To get away, they needed vehicles, but we're watching the roads. So how would they get past your roadblocks?"

"They didn't," Pete proclaimed.

"Then where are they? Where was he trying to run?" Mitch asked.

Two driveways to the west there was a mobile home with a carport. Two trucks and two cars parked and ready to pull onto the street. But no lights on inside. Not even the glow of a TV. Too early for anyone except the elderly and those souped-up trucks didn't belong to anyone who went to bed at seven at night.

Could it be that simple? He didn't wait to explain himself. He didn't wait to follow procedure. Or the letter of the law. Or wait for backup.

He jogged along the side of the road, hanging close to the edge of the pavement because of the darkness. He heard the squawk of the radio behind him. He'd dropped Hardy's a long time ago. He patted his pockets. No jacket meant no cell or extra clips. But the cold steel of a gun was secure against his back.

He skirted the wall of the mobile home. Listening. The front of the trailer had a direct line of sight to his fight at the tunnel. They probably knew their battle was lost.

"Mitch," Brandie whispered directly behind him. "Pete said to wait on him."

"No. Go back and give him my answer. This is too dangerous."

"I'm staying. This is Toby."

He knew that look and heard the determination in her voice. She couldn't kill him with niceness—he wasn't a customer, but she would be stubborn.

"Stay here. I'm going to the front door." He squeezed her hand. "They might not know my face, hon. Please stay here."

"Since you said please."

He saw all her hope that Toby was inside that trailer. Maybe he recognized it because he felt every bit as anxious for all of it to be over. If he weren't here...

Mitch turned the corner of the trailer and lightly stepped on the wooden porch leading to the door. The little glass panels used for the windows were raised. Whoever was inside could hear him.

"Toby, son," he raised his voice. "Can you hear me?"

"Go away," said a heavily accented woman. "No want."

"All I want is the boy."

"No boy here. Go away," she said.

"It's over." Brandie's eyes searched his from the corner. Pleading. "You don't want to hurt the *niño*. Just send him out and that'll be it."

He'd lie if it got Toby out of there. *What if you're wrong? What if they've already left and you're wasting time?* He could see the same questions in Brandie's movements.

A county vehicle, lights flashing, stopped about fifty feet away. Cord stood behind the door, the radio mic in his hand. "Rosita Morales, we know you're holding a little boy. Send him out to the officer, then follow with your hands up. If anyone's inside with you, have them do the same."

Cord said it in English for everyone to hear and then again in flawless Spanish. Before he finished the second time, the door creaked open. At Mitch's position on the short porch, he was trapped behind the door. He saw the joy and relief on Brandie's face and heard the running down the steps. It was Toby.

Chapter Twenty-Six

Each of Toby's feet hit the big steps, and he ran across the stepping stones the same way. He had a big, laughing smile on his face and didn't seem scared or abused. Brandie wanted to run to him, but Pete held her back, weapon drawn and pointed at the door.

She scooped her son into her arms, and Pete pushed them behind him, away from the mobile home and into another county vehicle farther down the street. He tapped on the hood, the car was put into gear and they left. She didn't see how everything ended. She didn't care.

Toby was chattering away. Brandie wanted to listen to him, concentrate on his words, but she stared at Sadie and the man who'd kept her son. They were facedown, hands cuffed behind their backs by the tunnel entrance.

Defeated.

"Are you okay, sweetie heart?" she asked.

"You had to work a long time, Mommy. I want to stay with Gramma Ollie next time. 'Kay?"

"Sure thing, absolutely."

"Ma'am?" Deputy Hardy interrupted. "We'd rather proceed to the station unless you think Toby needs a doctor."

"He seems fine. Why the police station?"

"We don't know what—if any—retaliation there might be. My orders are to protect you and the boy."

"Thank you."

Toby was safe, but the apprehension wouldn't leave her alone. Mitch was still there. He'd been behind the door when she'd left. They hadn't acknowledged any goodbye. If something happened...

But nothing was going to happen. He was just as safe as they were. She had to hold on to that thought, concentrate on Toby. She held her five-year-old so securely in her lap that he wriggled to be free.

"Too tight, Mommy."

"I'm just so happy to see you again." She wiggled her nose against his, unable to get enough of him. She was relieved, grateful, thankful.

"It's okay. I had an all right time. But I like my room."

"Sure you do." She kissed his forehead. He even smelled clean, like soap.

The deputy drove the two miles to the Presidio Police Station and escorted them both inside to the chief's office. A local officer stood outside the door as if they were fugitives. But they weren't.

One by one the Queen's men paraded by her. When the man Mitch had fought with staggered past, Toby smiled and waved. The man may have worked for a drug smuggler, but he'd obviously treated her son with kindness.

She heard Sadie coming through the main doors before she saw her. The expensive shoes were back on her feet. Brandie rubbed the side of her head where one had hit her during their fight. The leather skirt had been ripped and there was dried grass stuck throughout her long hair. She couldn't flip it and be beautiful. Her horrible true nature oozed out, screaming with every foul word that escaped her lips.

Then she saw Brandie. Her eyes darted to Toby drawing at the desk. She smiled by tilting the corners of her mouth and narrowing her eyes. It was so evil Brandie had to turn away. She wanted to protect Toby, to get him out of a building where this vile woman would be.

They couldn't leave. Mitch hadn't come through the doors.

She lifted Toby and sat him in her lap. She couldn't see the door, which made her even more nervous. Was he walking through it or on his way to a doctor?

"What are you drawing there, Toby?"

"See, this is the black tunnel we had to crawl through. Not really crawl, but they saids I could pretend. Mommy, I didn't get to brush my teeth. You aren't mad, are you?"

"No, no, honey, I'm not mad."

"Javier said you wouldn't be, but I didn't know for sure because of the mean lady." He touched her chin, drawing her attention to his wide-eyed baby blues. "I love you, Mommy."

She kissed his forehead again. She'd never get enough of his sweet smell and loving arms. She buried her face in his little neck until he giggled. "Toby Quinn Ryland, I love you right back."

"So do I."

"Mitch!" Toby jumped off her neck and ran to be scooped up into her knight's arms.

Not that horrible woman's knight. No, Mitch was hers. She knew she wanted to spend the rest of her life with him. The question was, did Mitch want a life with a ready-made family?

"The supposed Queen involved her mother, Rosita, and other family members. They're bringing in quite a few from her operation including the young women from this afternoon. All in all, I think we made a pretty good team out there." Mitch shifted Toby to his side and held out a hand to her. "Come on, let's get out of here."

Sitting handcuffed to a chair, Sadie didn't look as important or threatening any longer. "You know she really did think of herself as the Queen. She said her whole operation was thrown off because of the unknown variable of Toby's kidnapping. She is a horrible person."

"Don't think you're safe, Brandie. You'll never be completely safe," she spat from the other side of the room.

"Pipe down," an officer said, dropping the duffel of cocaine on his desk.

Brandie was no longer nervous. Her family was safe and they'd stay that way. She was never a person who spoke her mind, but this time, she had something to say.

"You should probably be more worried about yourself. You're a captured Queen. And I think you're wrong. I'm not your passed pawn to be traded for a more important piece. I'm on the winning side." Brandie didn't flinch when Sadie threw herself forward, attempting to stand. "I think that's checkmate."

Chapter Twenty-Seven

Toby fussed about having to take a second bath, but then Mitch said he'd take one, too, right after his mom. So they'd played with the toy soldiers and dinosaurs marching in two by two formation on the racetrack carpet. Toys and carpet had been moved to the living room so Bud and Olivia could enjoy the fun, too.

Once they were all clean, they ate grilled cheese sandwiches and tried for the best chocolate milk mustaches. Olivia and Brandie tucked Toby in bed, giving Mitch time to speak with Bud on the porch.

"You spending the night again, Ranger?"

"Yes, sir. I don't think she needs to be alone."

"You're right about that. I guess you'll be moving on to your next assignment then?" Bud stretched, smiling like a man with a secret.

"Actually, Bud, I, um…"

"You want to hang around here awhile?"

"If she'll have me, sir. Yes."

He clapped him on the shoulder. "I don't think there's a question about that. You take good care of them or you'll answer to me."

"Yes, sir. I know."

"Come on, Ollie. I'm yearning for a good night's sleep."

Mitch secured the doors, checked over the windows so

they'd both sleep sounder. While Brandie dried her hair, he pulled the couch cushions and stood them behind Toby's door. He took the blanket and pillows off the bed, looking at it longingly, imagining what might actually happen there one day.

But not tonight.

The drier went off as he pulled the covers back over Toby.

"He still asleep?" she asked from the doorway.

"I think he'll sleep at least until six, maybe six-thirty if we're lucky. You ready to hit the hay?"

"Yeah, but I don't think—"

"Brandie, I can't—" They both began, both grinned. "Check out behind the door. I sort of thought you'd want to stay in here, too."

They pushed the cushions together and leaned against the pillows. He was ready to wrap his arm around her when she pulled back, taking a deep breath and letting it out on a long sigh.

"I love you." She closed her eyes and leaned her head on his shoulder. "Not just for everything you've done in the past couple of days. It happened months ago. After one of those long, protective looks you gave me standing in the doorway to the garage."

"I think I've loved you since I met you. I never saw anyone after you and I honestly felt more at home on the cot in the garage than I have in years anywhere else."

"If you stay, will you still be a Texas Ranger?"

"I don't think they'll let me run the garage in my spare time, so no."

"Is that going to bother you?" she whispered.

"No. I like working on engines. And I like washing dishes after a bus has come through town. But there's a bigger question, Brandie... Will you marry me?"

"Absolutely."

Mitch pulled her across his body, their mouths sparking a passion he didn't think possible with anyone else. But not tonight.

He wrapped his arms around her body, keeping her close, watching for shadows. She rested her head on his shoulder, and he wrapped a hand in the long silky locks. He softly kissed her good-night, thinking about how good they'd be together. But that was their future.

Tonight was the first as a family.

Epilogue

Five weeks later

Brandie opened the door to the café, expecting business as usual. Toby ran through while she waited on Mitch a few steps behind them.

It was their first day back since returning from their honeymoon, and she'd been apprehensive about getting back to normal. Her parents had convinced them to sleep late. They'd open up like they had for the past week and take in Toby home with them when they swapped places.

"Surprise!" Multiple shouts and waving hands, then laughter and loud conversations.

It was standing-room only in the café. The bar was full of cake, sandwiches, a punch bowl and behind it stood her mom and dad. Her father had his arm around her mom, looking very proud and happy.

"Oh, my gracious," Honey and Peach said in unison. "You two should have seen your faces."

"I thought I was seeing double. It's so unusual for you sisters to be together and away from the sheriff's office. Who's minding the dispatch desk if you're both here?" Brandie hugged them both. "Thank you for coming."

"We couldn't miss it. We're so glad there's nothing wrong with Toby. He thought it was a sleepover. That's great. Just great." The sheriff's department dispatchers faded into the crowd.

Mitch wrapped his arms around her waist and whispered in her ear, "I think you have some friends, Mrs. Striker."

"I'm so very lucky." She did feel very lucky that there had been no lasting effects from the kidnapping. She turned her face to his, giving him a quick kiss. "And so are you."

"It's after the fact, but the two of you took off so suddenly to get married, no one had a chance to give you a shower. Or a reception, so surprise." Andrea explained the party faster than Brandie could take it all in.

Neighbors, friends and café patrons crowded more to the edge of the room, leaving a path straight to the far wall. "I can't believe it." Brandie ran to the shiny, refurbished jukebox. "You all shouldn't have. It was much too expensive."

"We didn't," Kate said, nodding to Mitch on the other side of the room. She handed her two shiny quarters. "Bride's choice."

Brandie's hands shook, but she got the coins through the slot. Her vision was blurry from happy tears, but she found her favorite song. She dabbed at the corner of her eyes and then extended her arms in an invitation. Her husband of one week wrapped her tightly and kissed her to a round of "awws."

They danced to her favorite song with only Toby talking in the background. The other couples swayed, but it was mainly them. It really was the reception she'd dreamed about. Held in her favorite place, with her favorite people.

At the next song everybody danced with them. Her dad dug the next quarters out of the cash register to keep the music going.

"I can't believe you got the jukebox fixed," she said to her husband during the next slow dance.

"I might even buy you those expensive sunglasses if you don't behave." He winked, then held her closer. He nibbled her neck. Something they'd both discovered she loved. "Do you get the impression that Toby isn't all that excited to see us?"

Toby was sitting on a bar stool, turning back and forth, but not spinning. He knew that was against the rules. "He's upset about something."

"Let me try." Mitch led her to the bar. "Hey, kid, why the long face?"

"Gramma Ollie said I need to wait."

"If there's a problem, then you should probably tell your old man. That'd be me now."

"I want a new name like Mommy."

"Well, now. That's not a problem. Your present came while we were on our trip. We've got papers at home to prove your name is now Toby Ryland Striker." Mitch announced the news of the adoption loud enough that her parents heard. They both stopped and hugged each other.

"For real?" Toby said with a brilliant smile, completely happy again.

"Want me to tell everybody for you?" Mitch asked.

"Naw," he whispered. "I think we need to eat cake."

"You got it." Mitch messed up Toby's hair, then smoothed it back down.

"I love you more and more every day," she told him. "You truly are my shining knight. Think you can keep that up for a while?"

"Sounds like the plan of a lifetime."

* * * * *

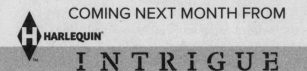
#1557 REINING IN JUSTICE
Sweetwater Ranch • by Delores Fossen
When his ex-wife, Addison, turns to him to recover her kidnapped newborn daughter, Sweetwater Springs deputy Reed Caldwell will do whatever it takes to find the child he never knew was his—and the love he thought he'd lost...

#1558 KILLSHADOW ROAD
The Gates • by Paula Graves
A by-the-book former operative, Nick Darcy may have to break all the rules to keep FBI Agent McKenna Rigsby alive. Eight years hasn't changed the chemistry between them, and staying ahead of the dangerous killers means staying very close to each other...

#1559 KANSAS CITY COVER-UP
The Precinct: Cold Case • by Julie Miller
Critical of the KCPD, reporter Gabriel Knight reluctantly joins forces with detective Olivia Watson to solve his fiancée's unsolved murder. With more than one criminal determined to keep the past buried, falling in love with the enemy has never been so dangerous.

#1560 SWAT SECRET ADMIRER
The Lawmen • by Elizabeth Heiter
FBI SWAT agent Maggie Delacorte's hunt for her rapist sends her into the arms of teammate Grant Larkin and the net of a cunning predator. If Grant can help Maggie lay her past to rest, will she be ready to take a chance on love?

#1561 AGENT UNDERCOVER
Special Agents at the Altar • by Lisa Childs
FBI special agent Ash Stryker poses as former hacker Claire Molenski's boyfriend to protect her from suspected spies. Can he keep her safe long enough for their fake relationship to become real?

#1562 MANHUNT • by Tyler Anne Snell
When Sophia Hardwick thrusts herself into detective Braydon Thatcher's investigation, Braydon must try to ignore his mounting attraction to her and find her missing sister—while keeping her out of the sights of a brilliant madman.

REQUEST YOUR FREE BOOKS!
2 FREE NOVELS PLUS 2 FREE GIFTS!

HARLEQUIN®

INTRIGUE®

BREATHTAKING ROMANTIC SUSPENSE

YES! Please send me 2 FREE Harlequin Intrigue® novels and my 2 FREE gifts (gifts are worth about $10). After receiving them, if I don't wish to receive any more books, I can return the shipping statement marked "cancel." If I don't cancel, I will receive 6 brand-new novels every month and be billed just $4.74 per book in the U.S. or $5.24 per book in Canada. That's a savings of at least 14% off the cover price! It's quite a bargain! Shipping and handling is just 50¢ per book in the U.S. and 75¢ per book in Canada.* I understand that accepting the 2 free books and gifts places me under no obligation to buy anything. I can always return a shipment and cancel at any time. Even if I never buy another book, the two free books and gifts are mine to keep forever.

182/382 HDN F42N

Name _____ (PLEASE PRINT)

Address _____ Apt. #

City _____ State/Prov. _____ Zip/Postal Code

Signature (if under 18, a parent or guardian must sign)

Mail to the **Harlequin® Reader Service:**
IN U.S.A.: P.O. Box 1867, Buffalo, NY 14240-1867
IN CANADA: P.O. Box 609, Fort Erie, Ontario L2A 5X3
**Are you a subscriber to Harlequin Intrigue books
and want to receive the larger-print edition?
Call 1-800-873-8635 or visit www.ReaderService.com.**

* Terms and prices subject to change without notice. Prices do not include applicable taxes. Sales tax applicable in N.Y. Canadian residents will be charged applicable taxes. Offer not valid in Quebec. This offer is limited to one order per household. Not valid for current subscribers to Harlequin Intrigue books. All orders subject to credit approval. Credit or debit balances in a customer's account(s) may be offset by any other outstanding balance owed by or to the customer. Please allow 4 to 6 weeks for delivery. Offer available while quantities last.

Your Privacy—The Harlequin® Reader Service is committed to protecting your privacy. Our Privacy Policy is available online at www.ReaderService.com or upon request from the Harlequin Reader Service.

We make a portion of our mailing list available to reputable third parties that offer products we believe may interest you. If you prefer that we not exchange your name with third parties, or if you wish to clarify or modify your communication preferences, please visit us at www.ReaderService.com/consumerschoice or write to us at Harlequin Reader Service Preference Service, P.O. Box 9062, Buffalo, NY 14269. Include your complete name and address.

HI13R

SPECIAL EXCERPT FROM

HARLEQUIN

I N T R I G U E

*What's an undercover agent to do when an injured
woman shows up on his doorstep and collapses before
she can tell him why she's there?*

*Read on for a sneak preview of
KILLSHADOW ROAD,
the fifth book in Paula Graves's
heartstopping miniseries THE GATES.*

Nick Darcy woke to the sort of darkness that one found
miles from a big city. No ambient light tempered the deep
gloom, and the only noise was the sound of his heart
pounding a rapid cadence of panic against his breastbone.

Just a dream.

Except it hadn't been. The embassy siege had happened. People had died, some in the most brutal ways
imaginable.

And he'd been unable to save them.

He pushed the stem of his watch, lighting up the dial.
Four in the morning. Sitting up on the edge of the sofa,
he started to reach for the switch of the lamp on the table
beside him when he heard a soft thump come from
outside the cabin. His nerves, still in fight-or-flight mode,
vibrated like the taut strings of a violin.

Leaving the light off, he reached for his SIG Sauer
P229 and eased it from the pancake holster lying on the
coffee table in front of the sofa.

The noises could be coming from a scavenging raccoon venturing onto the cabin porch or the wind knocking a dead limb from one of the blight-ridden Fraser firs surrounding his cabin.

But between his years with the DSS and the past few months he'd been working for Alexander Quinn at The Gates, he knew that bumps in the night could also mean deadly trouble.

As he moved silently toward the front door, he heard another sound from outside. A soft thump against the door, half knock, half scrape.

There was no security lens set into the heavy wood front door of the cabin, a failing he made a mental note to rectify as soon as possible. He improvised, edging toward the window that looked out onto the porch and angling his gaze toward the welcome mat in front of the door.

The view was obstructed by the angle, but he thought he could make out a dark mass lying on the porch floor in front of the door.

He checked the gun's magazine and chambered a round before he pulled open the front door.

A woman spilled inside and crumpled at his feet.

Don't miss
KILLSHADOW ROAD by Paula Graves,
available in April 2015 wherever
Harlequin Intrigue® books and ebooks are sold.

www.Harlequin.com

JUST CAN'T GET ENOUGH?

Join our social communities
and talk to us online.

You will have access to the latest
news on upcoming titles and special
promotions, but most importantly,
you can talk to other fans about your
favorite Harlequin reads.

Harlequin.com/Community

 Facebook.com/HarlequinBooks

 Twitter.com/HarlequinBooks

 Pinterest.com/HarlequinBooks